**losing**

**people**

**Also by Thomas Baird**

# losing

THOMAS BAIRD

Harcourt Brace Jovanovich | New York and London

# people

Copyright © 1974 by Thomas Baird

Printed in the United States of America


Library of Congress Cataloging in Publication Data

Baird, Thomas P      1923–
  Losing people.

    I.  Title.
PZ4.B1665Lo  [PS3552.A39]      813'.5'4      74-5757
ISBN 0-15-153468-3


First edition

B C D E

**For Henry and Pat Alexander**

# one

christmas eve

It was the last moment before the holiday, right on the threshold, right at the edge: four o'clock, Christmas Eve. The crowd at the airport outside Newark packed the waiting rooms, the ticket counters, and the gates, and the public address system was so continually in use to announce arrivals and departures and messages that only disconnected phrases of the sugary Christmas music scheduled to play over it got through at one time: jingling sleigh bells interspersed with flight announcements, and both howled down by jet engines. People were entirely involved in their reasons for being there, naturally, in their own comings and goings, yet it was hard not to look and to listen when Hugo Kerenyi met his family. His holiday rhetoric, his air of splurge, his very person were all so over-life-size! He seemed so magnificently to realize in speech and gesture what everyone was supposed to be feeling. Strangers smiled, watching him, caught up in his life for an instant, sharing his elephantine glee.

He began to demonstrate when his daughter-in-law appeared on a ramp surrounded by other passengers, stepping carefully as she changed worlds from the big transcontinental plane to the concrete earth, watchful of her precious burden. Hugo raised his arms and waved both of them, canceling out everyone else's signals. "Here. Here. Over here," he called. He pushed forward. "Jeanette, I'm over here." They came together: she pretty and a little pale from travel, timidly smiling, wearing a coat of pastel tweed with a fur collar, a little too light for the place and this season, the coldest Christmas in years; he, more than a foot taller, bending as he had to do to greet most people, but turning it into a bow, a distinction, looking like the officer of some kind of honor guard, with his brush of iron-gray hair and his wide shoulders, dashing, still a handsome man. He hugged her effusively but delicately, with no crush at all, only a little pressure of his forearms, keeping a distance. "What a splendid occasion! The best of Christmas this year is just this moment, for me. The very first is the best, I swear it to you. The very best. Even the Newark Airport has been enchanted for me by our being together in it at last." He pointed to an arrangement of plastic and foil ornaments, smiling ironically, one bushy eyebrow elevated, his blue eyes merry, yet, as she sensed, investigating her, noting things. "See how the walls have been hung with golden trophies and precious stones, Jeanette?" He kissed her, bending around the baby she carried, then backed off to take a good look at it. He dropped his voice. "And this is little Victoria, the latest bud upon the stem of my house. Delicious, I would say objectively. An edible shoot. I'll spirit her away, she is so charming. Thou lovely child, come go with me. No? She does not look as if she wants to. What a solemn face for eleven months—have I the age right? Good." He wobbled the baby's nose between his right thumb and forefinger; she stared at him from her mother's arms, but then suddenly smiled and so did he. When he saw his son, one of the last off, carrying baby's things, he bellowed his name, "Franz! Franz!" waving and shouting until he was sure he was seen. Then he waited, moved and solemn this time—a telling use of contrast, yet not necessarily all that self-conscious. The short, stocky, redheaded young man came closer, looking more drawn from travel than his wife, perhaps a little peevish, anyway not smiling as much or as easily, so it seemed, as his huge father. Hugo took both his son's hands. "Welcome, Franz." Silently, he looked down into the blue eyes, almost the only feature common to the two, until Franz swayed his head uneasily. Hugo suddenly burst out laughing. "How can I say welcome to Newark? Or to New Jersey? Both are just too—ignoble for this occasion."

"What will you say, then, Father?"

"Welcome to my presence. How's that? It has been far, far too long. Too long in time even for the long distance, and that, too, is too long."

"Such intervals are facts of life," Franz said.

"I have no patience with either time or space," said Hugo.

Franz smiled at that, just a little. He glanced around. "Mother stayed at home." It was neither a question nor a simple declarative.

"Oh, yes. She doesn't like to ride with me, and it's a boring drive up here."

"No worse than the flight from California."

Hugo looked around at the dense crowd. "Now I'll be your icebreaker. Ugh! Slushbreaker, rather." He plowed a path for them toward the place where they would get their luggage. "Here's a real collective proletarian experience for you, Franz; the world one would avoid," he remarked, when it seemed as if even he could not get through the glut of bodies at the turn of a corridor. He did, though, and while they waited, he talked exhaustingly about the systems used for handling luggage all over the world, as if he could thereby make the suitcases arrive faster, make Newark measure up. When they had everything, he managed to get a porter to help carry it to the outer doors (though they didn't really need one, and having one was really more trouble than not) while he got the automobile and brought it around to the entrance of the terminal, sounding his horn to make sure they saw him coming, the little family, and were ready to throw the suitcases and baby's traveling things into the trunk and jump in up forward themselves.

Then he drove them onto the turnpike, where he lunged and swerved through the holiday traffic, going seventy-five miles an hour whenever he could, one hand off the wheel most of the time, talking, talking, talking, about the places they passed, their ugliness mostly, about the history profession and the university, and above all, once he got around to it, about East Germany, where he had been last summer, largely in Weimar, the city of Goethe, Weimar and Goethe, Goethe and Weimar, together, now, his great interest. It was a terrifying demonstration of his inattentive and reckless driving to Jeanette, who sat in the back seat hugging little Victoria, alert to cover the tiny body with her own if there was an accident and she had time. She began to cry, noiselessly, to conceal it from her dour husband and from her father-in-law, and wished more than ever that she hadn't had to come, dreading her destination and frightened by the way she was being taken there. Her only earlier visit to the Kerenyi house had been in the springtime, when she and Franz were first engaged, nearly five years before; yet after they turned off the turnpike at New Brunswick and onto another highway and then at last reached the eastern side of Princeton, she recognized it, sitting at the end of its short street, could sense those parts she couldn't see, sense it all there, just as it had struck her that other time, big and overbearing, like her father-in-law himself, and like him alien to her in style and ideas, and old-fashioned, not what she wanted for herself in either case. Franz looked at it curiously, his head turning as the car turned into the driveway on the far right. He leaned back to see around his father. It was now after six, yet the house was dark. But not entirely. There was a light on in Miriam Kerenyi's sitting room at the left front corner of the second floor. Pale rectangles of it showed through the shades and draperies; and another light burned more brightly through the dormer window of the room just above Mrs. Kerenyi's, on the third floor. Only those two. Scarcely festive, the big, somber house, with sad, shaggy evergreens crouched close around the foundations, the two bare pin oaks in front, one thing darker and more lifeless than another—the frozen grass which no near change of season would quicken, the brittle forsythia canes scratching at them as they drew up along the driveway toward the garage.

"Ann's not here yet, I guess," Hugo said. "It's all right. They may have run into more snow after she telephoned that they'd been held up. I told them to fly. I told them those mountains in western Pennsylvania are always risky. I certainly expected they'd be here by now. Miriam hasn't thought to turn on the lights. Just imagine that, knowing everyone was coming!" He glanced quickly at his son, then back at his daughter-in-law. "That's how she is now, Jeanette. Of course, she always did like it darker than most people. Even in the days when she was always giving parties—seven parties in seven days one time—a perfect score—I kept count; it was too much for me—even then there were never a lot of lights on. Coral Pinckney—she's a friend of the family—you'll meet her tomorrow if you didn't before—Coral once said that coming to Miriam's Wednesdays was like going into a movie after the feature had started, that it took you five minutes to find out who was sitting next to you, and by that time it was too late." He laughed. "I'm completely different. I'd like to have every light on there is, even when I'm not in the house or likely to be. I just like the idea that it's all bright, just the way I like the idea that a person's life may be informed by reason." He laughed again. "Or say I do. Well, it's all right. A small thing, certainly. But wait here. I won't have you enter a dark house."

He got out and ran up the front steps and unlocked the front door and then, as the younger Kerenyis watched, lights came on quickly, one after the other, in the downstairs hall, then the upstairs hall and the landing in between, and lamps in the main living room over on the left, and one in the small living room to the right, forward of the dining room.

Hugo said, when he returned to the car, "That's enough. You aren't allowed to see *it* on, don't you know, until later, when the festivities officially start. It's all right, I say. Dorcas isn't expected until after the rush-hour traffic, and Ann and the family will surely be here any minute. Come on in. It's all right."

They had hardly started to get their luggage out of the trunk before Ann Kerenyi, now Ann Cuttler, and her husband, Bruce, and their children, William, aged eight, and Lucy, six, did arrive, in a big station wagon whose green sides were powdered with dried highway chemicals. Then there were many greetings and a great deal of bustle and confusion, unpacking the cars and all the rest, giving just the feeling that Hugo most liked: a sense of many people living lots of life around him. "Come on, come on. Hurry up there, Franz. Get inside the door, Annie." He herded them into the front hall. "Leave your packages here and I'll put them under the tree later. Now, all of you listen to the most important instruction," he said. "We will assemble in the living room at seven-thirty, which gives you only about an hour. Not much time for tired travelers to revive. And I'm going to take pictures, so look your best. No objections. I am. Your innkeeper must now show you upstairs to your rooms. Franz, I've put you and Jeanette in your own room in back, and I've set up the old crib and put two electric heaters in the room over the garage for little Victoria. You can open the door between her and you, if you like, but it will be very quiet, for her and so for us, I think. You know the way, so I'll let you take care of yourselves. The Cuttlers go to the third floor. Come along, Ann, and I'll introduce you to the student who is living with us this year. She'll be sharing the bathroom with all of you Cuttlers, the poor thing. Everybody take luggage, including the children. Hoist away, Billy."

Before they separated in the upstairs hall, Franz asked in a very low voice, "What about Mother?"

Hugo stopped. "I'm afraid I'm not really surprised."

"But shouldn't we . . . ?"

"I don't know."

Ann joined them, and her brother said to her, "We can't just walk past her door, can we, Annie? Her lights were on. She must have heard us arrive."

"Ergo," Hugo said, "we must suppose she is exercising a perfectly conscious choice."

Ann said, "Perhaps it's better to let her do things her own way, Franz."

Franz said querulously, "For me it's been four years, you know."

Hugo shrugged, rounded the newel post, and put a foot on the first step of the next flight, but stopped when Franz approached the door to his mother's sitting room, a hand raised, hesitantly. "If you want to, go ahead," Hugo said. "Try if you like. Annie and I may be wrong. It might be a good idea, not just—" He finished more emphatically. "Not just to give in to this." But Franz didn't knock. He turned back and took his baby and his wife to their quarters at the rear of the house.

Hugo led the Cuttlers to the third floor, where they were met at the top of the stairs by the roomer, a faintly exotic-looking girl of about twenty-three or -four, with very dark eyes and hair, and a thin face with prominent cheekbones. "This is Monique Lupiac." Hugo spelled it. "Her father is French, translated into American, and her mother is part Iranian."

As she shook the girl's hand, Ann Cuttler said, "Father has to trumpet your lineage to the world, it seems."

"Yes, to the whole world," Hugo shouted. "Her father is an Albigensian from Languedoc, and her mother is a descendant of Xerxes, and she is everything kind and wonderful. She could not go home because they're in—is it Ankara, at our embassy in Ankara?—so the Kerenyi Christmas is partly her Christmas this year, is her Christmas for tonight, and that is your good luck, because she is an angel and she will help you with the children when she's needed, which is right now, I suspect. That's the children's room, and that is yours. See? She takes them away already and leaves you free, you two. Bruce, you know all about the facilities and possibilities of this floor, more I dare say than I ever will, so now I'll leave you."

But Ann raised again the question of Miriam Kerenyi. "I can't help but wonder if Mother really wouldn't like us, really doesn't want us, to barge in on her, the whole crowd of us, all at once."

"My opinions turn out so often to be wrong I no longer offer them."

Ann looked thoughtfully at him, started perhaps to argue, but, like her brother, changed her mind. "It's very awkward," she said, "and unnatural."

"Very," Hugo replied, with a kind of sad satisfaction.

"I don't mean it that way." Hugo was leaving, and Ann was speaking to his departing back. "I mean the effect she's getting. It's too—oh, somehow too stagey. Do you see?"

"Now you're raising other questions," her father replied from halfway down the stairs.

He disappeared, and Ann went to turn the water on and fill the bathtub. Not only would it take a little time to get the water to run hot, this far away from the heater in the basement, but also she well remembered from earlier years that the last person to draw a bath in the house was likely to take it in cold water. After driving so far, she wasn't going to take any chances.

The Kerenyi house had been designed for holidays and feasting as well as for comfortable day-to-day living, for large families and for big family gatherings of just this kind: a house of many rooms, built for plural conversations, for confidences and gossip and even for intrigue. Not that it was a mansion. It was just an ample, sixty- or seventy-year-old house, in a half-timbered style, probably built to be fashionable though now in an unfashionable part of Princeton; yet it had a kind of inelegant delight about it with its irregular plan, its alcoves and window seats and absurd leaded casements, and all stuffed full as it was of hand-me-down furniture and small objects from both Kerenyi and Baxter sources.

The hour before the company assembled was a busy one for Hugo, who had to ready his house, complete all the arrangements before the traditional family Christmas Eve could begin. He refined the lighting on the Christmas tree ("it," as he had referred to it), a job which, as always, caused him to rage when the strings wouldn't look as he wanted them to, and gave him extreme satisfaction when they did. He left it, however, still disconnected when he had finished, and tucked the cords and plugs under the green felt covering that was spread out to conceal the raw base of the tree and catch falling needles from the boughs. He also put wine in the refrigerator to cool, lots of it, in slender green bottles with long necks, and removed the food that should come to room temperature and set it on the cream-painted wooden counters of the big pantry. Then he finished setting out china and silver and glasses, and after that he diagramed on a piece of paper the way everyone was to be placed at supper, standing at the buffet in the dining room as he wrote in order to be able to visualize what he was doing. He made a puzzle out of the seating, of who should go where and why, and dawdled for ten minutes while he recalled suppers of the past, when there had always been many more present—friends of different generations, and colleagues, and visitors to town. By the time he had followed down these many pathways of memory, it was seven-thirty.

Ann Cuttler, dressed in a long canary-yellow skirt (a color her mother never wore), her fine brown hair coiled up high on her head to show off her striking necklace of cloisonné plaques, was ready a little early, and sat at the dressing table in the third-floor bedroom, waiting while her husband stood behind her inserting his cufflinks. In the end, he had to bring the left one to her to do, for he was very left-handed. Then he put on his coat and regarded himself in the mirror above the dresser and was not displeased with what he saw. Ann watched him. She was used to it, but here, in this house, this evening, she was reminded of a keen remark Miriam Kerenyi had made of him years before: he could have made a career of his good looks, but it never would have satisfied his vanity. Together, then, he and Ann collected their children from Monique, releasing her to finish getting ready, and went downstairs where Franz Kerenyi joined them, and then a little later Monique came down herself, so that by the time Dorcas Baxter, Miriam's unmarried sister, arrived from her school outside Philadelphia at twenty minutes before eight, the household was complete, except for Jeanette and Miriam. Aunt Dorcas, as she was called by everybody in the family, left her overnight bag and coat in the hall and brought a big Wanamaker's shopping bag, filled with presents, into the living room. After she had greeted them all, which she did in a style as disparate as imaginable from Hugo's—the children had to be lifted to her by Ann, to be touched lightly by her lips well away from anywhere wet and germy—she piled her parcels, which were wrapped identically in white tissue paper and silver ribbon, upon the ones already under the tree, the mound of brightly colored cubes and oblongs which now included the contributions both of the younger Kerenyis and of the Cuttlers. That done, Aunt Dorcas stood up, straight and severe in her knee-length dark-brown flannel dress with those usual superfluous rows of buttons on sleeves and bodice, looked around, noticed that everyone was watching her, sensed a kind of constraint over them, became self-conscious, and broke the silence by a banality.

"Well, here we are," she said.

"Yes, here we are," said Hugo.

"One big happy family," she said.

Hugo erupted. "All one big happy family." He filled the whole house with his loud voice. "One big happy family. Good for you, Aunt Dorcas." When he saw her flush a little and look down, feeling a fool, he went to her and clapped her shoulder. "Yours is the voice, the true voice of hope. I wonder if the person who invented that phrase knew what it meant. I wonder if he'd ever seen one. I wonder if there is such a thing." Hugo laughed. "I'm not making fun of the cliché. I'd never do that, for they embody, those worn phrases, the simple ideas we satirize only at our peril, don't they, eh? Only wondering what it really means." He addressed himself to his daughter. "I'm raising an important question. Happiness is, in its primary meaning, an emotional state possibly related to a material condition. Therefore it can be possessed in that primary sense only by individuals. Am I not right, Ann? Or do I get an instant contradiction from you about that, dear Sphinx? Is it correct to say, without much qualifying, that a group, a country, a century, is happy?" He was enjoying himself now, spinning out his verbal web, not even half serious, yet ready to plunge into real argument, and on either side, too, if anyone wanted to take him up on any part of it, to disagree or to agree too strongly. "Are not our applications of this word 'happy' to the inorganic and to abstract nouns, our constant metaphorizing—that's what it is—which is to say our not really thinking of the specific case itself, not finding therefore the descriptive terms proper to it, but thinking in parallels to which we liken the case unaware, thinking in lazy analogies, whereby our minds are set as much afloat, wiggling their toes upon thin air—I can see you, Aunt Dorcas, about to stop me to say that to endow a mind with wiggling toes is rhetoric quite inadmissible by the standards of the Ancients—as I was saying, wiggling their toes upon thin air as if we were mere philosophers—shouldn't those extensions of the word, Franz—a happy land, a happy century, a happy family—be struck from the historian's ever-shortening list of admissible abstractions?" Suddenly he did grow serious, it seemed, and more seriously magisterial. "I think such usages may be one of the ways in which we most mislead, Franz, we historians, and are by ourselves the most misled. Yes, we ring the hammer of metaphor upon the anvil of reification, attempting thereby to forge something meaningful out of . . . nothing! Precisely nothing."

"Whew!" exclaimed Bruce Cuttler.

Hugo looked at him blankly, as if he had not understood what he'd said, only knew he'd said something. "Hmmm. One big happy family. Well, I suppose ours doesn't do badly."

"But you're not big," Bruce said. "I had seven brothers and sisters. I call that big."

"Granted you were a big family. Tell us, were you happy?"

"More hungry than happy, I think."

"Hungry? Oh. I see. Well, this is no occasion to consider childhood deprivation, is it? Hungry . . . The others, perhaps, but not you, Bruce. You got enough, I'll bet." Hugo changed the subject. "Now for my photography. I'm going to get started right now. Everybody's here except Father and Jeanette. And Miriam. Where's Jeanette, Franz? Has she dozed off? Go at once and awaken her," he commanded, then, surprised himself by how harsh he had sounded, added, with a smile, "please."

"She's late because by the time I'd taken mine and she'd finished with the baby, there wasn't any hot water for her bath," Franz said. "Everybody else got there first."

Hugo was delighted. "Ann, of course. My foresighted Ann, who considers both the forest and the trees and the land beyond. Bruce, too? Yes, Bruce, too, naturally. She'd have seen to that."

Ann said, "If you wanted me to hold off, Franz, you should have paid me the necessary quarter."

"Wonderful, wonderful," Hugo cried. "See? Even our serious Franz must grin. We gave Ann priority on hot water, Bruce, because girls should be cleaner than boys, and if there was a question of running low and it didn't matter to her, she'd sell her rights to Franz when he was in a hurry, had a date, you know. Isn't that your capitalism at work? What a different picture of these two dignified, grown-up Kerenyis that presents, doesn't it? Engaged in commerce and diplomacy and sometimes even war over bath water. And what—what consolation is to be found in old family bones of contention, the rancor soothed by time. But this has not brought us Jeanette and Victoria."

"You should have warned us you expected Victoria for tonight's pictures, Father," Franz said. "She's had her bottle and is in bed."

"Oh, but she can't be."

"But she is. Take her tomorrow."

"No, really. This will be the only photography. I don't plan to inflict it on you tomorrow, and Victoria must be here. She will be the star. Really, she must be. Please, please," he begged, jokingly, because it was scarcely conceivable that he would not get his way. "Please, please, my son. I hear a car. That will be the oldest member of the family. And so, to balance him, we must have the youngest. Do go tell Jeanette to bring the baby down with her."

Franz started for the stairs, and Hugo went to open the front door for old Franz Kerenyi, whom one of the attendants had brought in from the country estate, now a home for the aged, where he lived—quite by his own wish. He did not want a room in his son's house; it had been offered him. He was, or had been, as tall as Hugo but less mas-

sively made, more finely knit, and like him had eyebrows
that circumflexed rather high over his blue eyes and tufted
out at their angles, and a great shock of hair, only his was
all white. It was crowned tonight with a black astrakhan
hat, and his overcoat, which was quite long, down almost
to his ankles, was lined with fur and had a fur collar, and
could not have come from any American store, nor could
his suit, which was of a heavy blue stuff, formally cut;
under it he wore a vest and stiff collar. It was a mildly
defiant costume, and seemed to serve notice that he was no
mere immigrant ape, eager to assume the manners and
modes of his adopted country.

"Merry Christmas, Father and Grand—and Great-grandfather. Come in, come in," Hugo cried. The old man
winced at the noise of his son's party manner, but with res-
ignation. "Give me your coat. The weight of it! How ever
do the little muskrats carry all that around? We've been
waiting for you, the patriarch of our tribe, our Abraham.
We can now proceed seriously to take photographs."

Old Mr. Kerenyi, his voice, like his smile, muted, said,
"Yes, yes. Photographs, by all means." He said hello to everybody else, deliberately and one by one, studying their
faces, and in particular paid special attention to Billy and
Lucy Cuttler, whom he had seen only two or three times
before, and who were shy and well behaved in the presence of such an intimidating ancestral figure.

Meanwhile Hugo got out his camera.

The chief entrance to the living room was off the hallway at the front end of the house. Opposite it, in the corner, placed to show to the street as well as to the room, was
the Christmas tree, its lights still not on. Hugo extended
the legs of his tripod, threaded the body of the camera onto
its mount, attached the flash, and set it up fairly close to
the doorway, so that he could take in the tree and space
around and in front of it. He corrected the focus, set the
aperture and speed adjustments, pulled some chairs over,

and explained to Monique how to be sure that nobody was left outside the frame and how to work the cable release and advance the film.

"If only everybody would get here." He looked at his watch. "It's eight o'clock. This is ridiculous. Ah, here's Franz back, at least. And here's Jeanette and the baby." Jeanette, her arms full of drowsy Victoria, came rather hesitantly into the room, staying close to the wall until Hugo propelled her forward. "This is Victoria, Father, the youngest of the Kerenyis," he said to the old man, who had seated himself near the piano in a straight-backed arm-chair, to wait.

Old Franz first reacquainted himself with Jeanette's face, then looked curiously at her bundle. "Another great-grandchild. Just think of that. She will be as pretty as you," he said to the mother, who then, at his request, handed the baby to him to hold.

Earlier, Hugo had placed a big silver tray on top of the piano, with ice and glasses and bottles of whisky and gin and vermouth on it. "We can't wait forever for our cock-tails, can we? Isn't this a bore! I'd expected to be finished with my snapshooting long since." He took orders and mixed them up and spilled soda and broke a glass and had to get more ice, but even he could not make sufficient clat-ter and fuss to gloss over Miriam's strange delay, now growing unpleasant, and on everybody's mind—includ-ing, indeed, above all, his, as was evident from the way he kept frowning at the doorway no matter how busy his hands were, and perhaps explained his letting the glass slip through his fingers to fall onto the piano lid.

Old Mr. Kerenyi could say what he liked. "Where is Miriam?"

"Dressing, dressing. It doesn't matter. It is a cold supper, all done in advance."

Aunt Dorcas said, "I drove all the way from King of Prussia and got here on time. I believe that punctuality and cordiality go together. We try to teach our girls that."

"And can't Mother live by other rules, Aunt Dorcas?" Ann chided her, smiling.

Hugo listened. There was no sound at all from above, although Miriam's rooms were directly over the living room, and in that old house movement was prone to translate itself into a creaking of floor boards. "Perhaps I had better go call her. I will. Yes, I will." He left.

Old Mr. Kerenyi had heard Dorcas's and Ann's exchange of remarks, but his consideration of them was delayed while he sat quietly, looking down at the baby, but thinking about its mother and father. A strange choice, that placid, childbearing young woman, for young Franz, himself so uneasy in his skin, so gruff yet timid, and never quite squarely behind his manner. An unpredictable mix: how would a child with such an inheritance turn out? He would never know. He glanced over at the Cuttler children. Or about them. He didn't really care. His mind caught on to the thread of their mother's remark, which had to do with things he did care about.

"You are too intelligent to believe what you said just now about rules, Annie," he whispered, so that no one else heard. "No, it isn't other rules. It is very bad with your mother."

"But why, Grandfather? What?"

He freed a hand and gestured, as if to wave it all away if he could. "I don't know. But it is not her illness of last year, I'm pretty sure of that. It was becoming this way before she was ill, and it is growing since then, too. Jeanette," he called, "come and take Victoria, please." As the mother did so he touched the infant's forehead with a finger whose nail was yellow and curved, and said something in German—a blessing, perhaps, the secular blessing of an agnostic, which can only wish well.

Hugo came back downstairs. "She is all ready and is following close behind me," he said.

"What was she doing?" Aunt Dorcas asked resentfully.

Hugo did not smile. "Nothing."

Aunt Dorcas said, "A lot of time to take to do that!"

Bruce Cuttler said, "That takes more time than anything else, Miss Baxter, as Hugo's historians prove."

"Nothing. Nothing. You see, Annie?" whispered Mr. Kerenyi.

"Not yet, Grandfather."

With a sudden clap of his hands Hugo got everybody's firm attention, so that he could start to arrange them for the photographing. The baby, startled, whimpered a little in Jeanette's arms, where she was now once more cradled. Hugo went over to her. "Excuse me, excuse me." He waggled a finger at her as big as one of her arms. "Nay, nay," he said. "Don't cry, Victoria. See? She stops at once. Her heart isn't in her tears. She is only reminding us that she can cry if she needs to. How charming her smile is! And Father is right. How pretty she will be, just like you, Jeanette. A peaches-and-whipped-cream baby, with honey and powdered sugar on her. And she is certainly possessed of my problematical happiness. Yes, a happy baby. Whereas Ann and Franz," he said, rearing to stare at them in a kind of mock outrage, "at her age were already vexed from wanting things whose names they did not yet even know."

"You set us an example," Ann said, smiling.

"Quite right, quite right. I have to admit that I am greedy for my own way," Hugo said, boasting the scale of his self. "Even, I am afraid, when that way is not directed toward the benefit of other people."

"Even when it is," said his father.

"Which is so often," said the quiet Monique Lupiac.

All the family turned to look at her over near the fireplace, where she sat on a couch, one Cuttler child held down by her hands on either side.

"More often than we'll admit," said Ann. She carried Monique a little dish of almonds, grateful that she was there to tend the children. "But often it's not the case, so don't be misled into—hero worship," she finished, and was sorry she'd hit on the term, which didn't seem quite appropriate: it was too extreme, not quite the right thing to have said.

Monique looked down, lowering her eyelids, dropping her head a little, as if embarrassed; but that wasn't at all sure, it could be a version of good manners: one knew about the Gallic, but what about the Iranian? Ann relieved her of the children by sending them to help Hugo, who had gone to arrange the presents under the tree into more photogenic patterns, sat down beside her, and asked her what kind of graduate student she was. History? One of Hugo's? Did they have women in all the departments at Princeton now? Monique was in International Affairs—the Woodrow Wilson School—almost a family business. Ann, while making conventional conversation about the university, then watched her father and her children, thinking of the dangerous power and seduction of his intellect, as she'd seen it work in the past—the way young men had to hunch down under it to endure its force, and often learned to resent it. As Bruce had. But a woman? Like this semiexotic intruder in the midst of the boisterous Kerenyi family, who was good enough to sit with the children on Christmas Eve? Why was she living in the house at all? Did she need money, for instance? Bruce could decide about a tip. Ann looked up at the ceiling, and then stood.

Announced by the floor boards overhead, and then by the stairs in the hallway outside, Miriam was at last coming to join her family. They could, by the noisy old stairs, chart her descent, too—never fast, sometimes hesitating—hear her foot on each step, hear that once she stopped and might have turned back—it was a possible interpretation—but then didn't. As she rounded the corner at the landing, the banister creaked when she leaned on it, which it had been doing beyond all memory. The family turned to face the doorway, Franz looking morose, Ann worried. Hugo, up front, stood, holding in his hands the electric cords he had just got out from under their felt cover, frowning in fierce concentration. Then at last there she was, and just as she appeared, Hugo jammed the main plug into a socket and the Christmas tree lights came on, all blue and green: no other colors, just blue and green, the way Miriam liked it.

Christmas had begun.

Miriam stopped. She stood at first, blinking with a kind of haughty uncertainty, as if she found ten people a great multitude, as if a little dismayed by a crowd in her living room. She raised a hand and rested it upon the jamb of the doorway but did not lean on it. Then, smiling, she looked around, yet not into the eyes of anyone, unconnecting, with something like that calculated vagueness of the actress who seems to look at everybody yet at nobody, a look across significant spaces and through divisive lights. Everyone else was in doubt, too, unsure; no one could be spontaneous; there was no chorus of loving greetings. There had been too much suspense, perhaps; everyone had been kept waiting too long for this moment. There was mere silence while she looked at them and they at her, except for a little stirring as old Mr. Kerenyi slowly got to his feet. Even young Franz, who had not seen her in so long, was silent. He felt it was up to her to single him out, as he had felt it was up to her to have come out of her room to speak to him earlier, when he arrived. To him, now, she looked much the same as ever—thin, but not different enough, since her illness, to excuse her neglect. Very thin, but yes, so much the same. She was still the dark lady of his childhood. She was and would always be as she had been then: cool, and slipping sideways as much as going forward, always just out of reach, eluding his touch yet supremely present, and—vivid, brighter than life, radiant, nimbed in wonder. As tonight, with a long dress on of blazing orange, and some kind of exotic red shawl over her shoulders, a juxtaposition of colors that dazzled alike the eye of boyhood's love and manhood's reproach.

The silence, the waiting, really lasted only a few moments. Monique glanced at Hugo. He had brought this to pass, but he would not break the spell. Now it was up to other people—to Miriam. Monique spoke, dared to speak.

"Merry Christmas, Mrs. Kerenyi."

"Ah, Monique." Miriam held her hands out to the girl, inviting her to come. "Merry Christmas to you, too." And thus it happened that it was none of the kin but rather the stranger in the house who received Miriam's first kiss.

After that Miriam did as one would have expected: she went first to Franz and Jeanette, and ceremoniously, not casually. She kissed her son, then held him at arm's length afterwards and, choosing just one aspect of their long separation to remark on, said, "It is the first time I've seen you since *Give Me Your Tired* was published. You don't look at all different, but I don't quite believe my eyes. I know you for a man who has added to his stature the thickness of a very distinguished book indeed." The remark was surely flattering, yes, and affectionate—except just possibly (how could one be sure that it was intentional?) for a little flick to its tip, in that Franz was the only short member of the Kerenyi family. When it was the baby's turn, Miriam looked carefully at her, spoke her name, pronounced her a good start at a family, but then turned away, just as if Victoria had no thick-blood connection with her, as if she were just any baby. After Great-grandfather's cuddling and Hugo's fuss, Miriam's very first look at her new granddaughter was certainly, well, perfunctory; and Jeanette, who had begun to think that this daunting holiday might not be so bad if only everybody just kept petting the worshipful Victoria, ended by wishing she'd refused to bring her back downstairs tonight—ended, as she hugged Victoria closer in desperate alliance, by becoming uneasy again, made so by the one person of all the group who, by rights, least ought to have done it.

Miriam may have sensed that she'd offended by falling short, because she turned back from the Cuttlers to say, "Now Jeanette, you must not go through life sending this soul to heaven and that one to hell according to how much attention they pay to your babies." She laughed, and it was wonderful to hear it again, to hear her laugh when she thought she was on target and had scored nicely. "I caught you, didn't I? Just imagine how disrupted the world would be if everybody did as you would like them to. Victoria's chin would be worn away from chucking, looking at it from her side, and from ours—well, nobody has more than just so much energy and attention to invest, and it wouldn't go around. Mine must now stretch to Ann and Bruce and Dorcas and Grandfather." Having named them, Miriam went to each one in that order, and the Cuttler children more or less in passing.

Hugo hardly let her finish. "There. That's done," he cried. "All of us are here together at last. Now for photography. I'm going to take you by the Christmas tree, so why don't you all close in over there. Good. Move a little to the left, Ann, so that your leg is touching the window seat. Let me look through the camera. Mmm. Just about right. Only let's loosen up. Franz, move a couple of feet to the right, to give me an idea of what it will be like when there are three chairs there. So. I'll just move the camera back a couple of paces." He moved back toward the doorway, carefully lifting the tripod and camera and resetting it. He tested its stability by jiggling it. "That's fine. Now then, we get to the furniture-moving." He stopped and thought. "Should we begin informally? Or with the royal birthday portrait? Let me think. Franz, do go and get the armchair your grandfather was sitting in, and bring it and put it right there where that medallion is on the rug. Right over it. That is where the patriarch will sit. We'll get him off his feet right away so that he won't be too tired to drink lots of wine, which has been selected particularly and solicitously with him in mind. Now the two side chairs there and there. They should go on either side of him." Hugo waited. "That is right. Now you go there, and Ann, you there, and the children down in front by the right of Grandfather, and next to Miriam. No, move to the other side and give yourself more room; and Jeanette, I think perhaps you had better sit on Father's right, and I'll stand behind you. Let me look. I don't like it. What can I do? Bruce, you might put your hand on Jeanette's shoulder. No, that's no good. It looks as if you were her husband and Victoria a credit to *your* loins that way. These damned family pictures are always so difficult. Oh, what the devil; it'll do. Father, turn a little to look at Lucy. And relax a bit. You look entirely too much like Franz-Josef. Smile, Miriam, or anyway look benevolent. Enough. Enough. Here, Monique. We'll take it this way."

Hugo got into it himself, and so that view was taken. And several others like it, with small variations. But that was only the beginning.

After that, Hugo had to have photographs of each of the subfamilies, and then of individuals, and then of cross-family groups, and Ann and Franz, Bruce and Jeanette, Miriam and old Franz; pictures, too, with Monique and without Monique, of Franz with his niece and nephew, Ann with delicious Victoria, Billy and Lucy Cuttler burrowing amongst the presents, and so on and on and on until it seemed it would never end, Hugo getting more and more excited and extravagant (and bored), flailing his arms, shouting, now irritated, now amused. It was a scene out of the family past, one that nullified time, a scene such as they had all experienced many times over, at least the close family, with Hugo Kerenyi organizing something, always organizing something, in the middle of it, it didn't matter what: a picnic, a birthday party, going swimming or to some kind of game at the stadium or the gymnasium, getting off to the shore for the summer, or, like this, taking pictures on a great occasion. All of them sat, stood, smiled, shuffled, and rotated in numb obedience the way they always had. They reverted: Ann to the leggy adolescent who found small ways of letting her father know what she thought generally of unreason in grownups, Franz to the undersized, rufous-headed boy with the distressing tendency to hide when he anticipated these family scenes, and Aunt Dorcas to the awkwardly accommodating spinster sister who, before she'd met her friend Hazel Glidden and begun to take vacations with her, had spent all her holidays and many of her weekends with the Kerenyi family because very often she didn't have anywhere else to go. It was a great strain, because not one of them longed for those good old days.

Ann had had more than one special privilege in the family; she could, for instance, safely say things Franz could not. She did so now. "Father, you have to stop."

"I won't. Why?"

"I can't stand it any longer. It's unbearable."

"What do you mean?"

"It's gone on too long. All your usual confusion and inefficiency, and we don't dare refuse to do what we're told. And anyway," she added, more gently, "we know it will all come out all right in the end, even though it hasn't always, because God is God and you are you." Hugo didn't know whether or not to be offended; he might have gone either way; but Ann continued quickly, not giving him the chance to choose wrongly. "I might begin to cry, it's so nostalgic. How we all hated it and loved it and we'll never live more excitingly, I suppose. Do you remember the day we climbed—what was it?"

Aunt Dorcas provided the precise name. "Old Raggedy Mountain is probably what you mean."

"Yes. Old Rag Mountain. In Shenandoah Park. You were with us, Aunt Dorcas. Do you remember that, Franz?

Mother, do you remember that day?" Ann looked for Miriam, who had drifted toward the back of the room, and caught her slow nod.

Hugo said, "Of course they all remember. A wonderful day in every way."

"A high point of your bossiness, that's sure. Deciding who would walk first and who last—though you, of course, went absolutely first yourself. Then he'd tell us—do you remember, Dorcas?—when to switch our marching order, and he'd check every scramble and slide for safety and lecture us about it; and he wouldn't let us blow our noses for fear we'd scare away the deer, and mine was running all the time with the tail end of a cold and I was miserable about that and wouldn't let anybody look straight at me, but he himself never stopped shouting and pointing out things for us to look at, and we never got near a deer, naturally."

"Now, no mutinies, sentimental or otherwise," Hugo said. "I can see from Billy's eyes that he wishes he'd been along and *he'd* have seen the flash of a whitetail, also that he is ravenous and so am I, and this *has* been going on far too long, and I'll give in. No more photography if you'll just let me take a final picture—of Ann and Bruce and Franz and Jeanette, all four together. It's one I'm missing." Hugo placed them. "There. That's very good. I'm struck, as I look at you, by how physically both my children have chosen—beautiful Jeanette, handsome Bruce. We will not stop now to wonder what it means. Smile. So. All right, everybody, photography is officially over. We will now turn our attentions to the poor meager supper I have provided—with some slight assistance from the morose but indispensable Mrs. Vendredy."

He removed the flash attachment, which stuck, and just had his hands on the tripod to close it so that he could unscrew the camera, when he noticed something. "Where is Miriam?" he asked sharply. "Franz, where is your mother?"

"How do I know?"

"We must find her."

Hugo went out into the hall and up the stairs at a trot, checked her rooms, and was back down in time to overtake young Franz, who, moving slowly toward the rear rooms, had stopped for more whisky and was just strolling into the library. Miriam was not there, but she could be seen standing in Hugo's private study, a small room off to the left, holding a book she had taken from the shelves.

"What are you doing, Miriam?"

She looked over, calmly. "Reading. Is all that finished, out there?"

"Reading? Reading?" Hugo was very angry. "You can't be reading on Christmas Eve."

"But Hugo, you can't disapprove of reading."

"Come now, Miriam, don't try to play your games with me. Your disappearances are embarrassing and unfair. Reading at such a time. During a family reunion. I won't have it."

She held up the book so they both could see its jacket. "Moreover, I was reading in Franzie's book."

"You can do that later. Come along now, both of you," Hugo said, walking out of the room quickly, not at all mollified, though it was hard to see why she shouldn't have strayed off for a few minutes. When he came to the waiting group, he said curtly, still angry, "She's found. Now we can all go in to table. Hurry up, hurry up. Come along," just as if it had not been he who had caused most of the delay.

Jeanette went to put the baby to bed, and the others moved in the direction of the front entrance, but let Miriam by to go first, with old Franz, who offered her his arm. She was almost out the door when she noticed the tree, just as if it hadn't been on ever since she had come downstairs.

"It is pretty this year, isn't it, Grandfather?" she said. "Hugo's very good at them. I'm afraid that sometime along the way I helped decorate one tree too many, but still they are pleasing, like everything improbable." She let go of old Mr. Kerenyi's arm and walked back, to stand a moment quite close to the tree, look right into its heart. "Yes, it is pretty." She backed up. "Two colors, neighbors on the rainbow, that's just right; nothing miscellaneous. And it's good and bushy. For what it is, Hugo, it's a triumph." She turned to walk toward the doorway and her father-in-law once more, still looking back at the tree, and knocked into the camera, which Hugo had never finished taking down. Over it went, with a crash.

"Father, your Leica," Ann cried.

Miriam stared down at what she had done. "Hugo, I really didn't mean to do that," she said.

"No matter, no matter," he mumbled. He picked it up, shook it, looked it over to see if anything was obviously broken, glanced at the rest of the family, but never looked at his wife. "I'll have to have it checked," he said, and leaned it up against the wall, still on the tripod. "After tomorrow."

Old Franz beckoned to Miriam to take his arm again. As she did so, Miriam said, "Perhaps the shaking—or breaking—it just got will turn it into a magic camera."

"Magic camera?" he asked, as they walked on into the hall, young Franz and Ann close behind.

"One you can use to photograph the—to photograph ghosts. Nicky, for instance. I thought of that just now. Why not include a vacant place for Nicky in one of our group pictures? Hugo is always talking about having a record of all of us; that would be a record, too, wouldn't it?"

Old Franz said, "If one began to take pictures of the dead, Miriam, there'd be no end to it. No end at all."

"But there seemed to be no end to photographing the living," she replied.

He smiled his small, careful smile. "No, no, I assure you, it's better this way." They came to a stop at the dining-room table. "One of the pleasures of . . . later will be no photography on holidays. And so, as for me, I absolutely forbid the use of any magic cameras when I am a ghost myself."

"That is the attitude of someone who has not been short in his years," Miriam replied, rather seriously.

"To be sure." The old man put his right hand on hers where it was crooked through the bend in his left arm, to indicate that they had said enough about all that. "Oh, yes, to be sure, that is quite true. But look, now. See all the star moss and partridge berry. And Hugo has got out the Meissen. Isn't it remarkable? Another Christmas Eve, and I still alive to participate, and to watch again while small children discover the pretty painted beetles and butterflies on their plates."

Another kind of Kerenyi family scene, it too with predecessors back through the years, back as far as either child could remember; back beyond even that, beyond Dorcas's recollections, to a first time, Hugo and Miriam newly married, feasting Franz Kerenyi on the vigil of Christmas; a long arc of time, rising, turning, and dropping again, into this present occasion . . .

Hugo grew genial in the dining room, his pet with Miriam forgotten, and with the geniality, loud and directorial. He got his seating chart from the pocket of his green velvet jacket, smoothed it out, put on his glasses, and began the placement. "Now, then . . . Father, you sit to Miriam's right, there. We're an odd number, so she's at the head of the table opposite me. That's right, Miriam. And Franz, you to her left. Aunt Dorcas, you are here by me, and Bruce there next to you. And Ann, you're up there, next to your grandfather, and Jeanette will be by me here when she comes down, and Monique, you there by Bruce, and little Lucy next to you and her Uncle Franz. So that leaves only you, Billy, and unless I've mixed something up you are in the only seat which remains, and that is the one there between your mother and your aunt. And that is that. Has everybody got it straight? Get behind your chairs, all of you, so I can see how it looks. Jeanette," he said, when she reappeared at that moment, "I did the plan and as you will see, have claimed the reward of the labor: you are right here by me." The family shifted around to their places. "Now all of you sit down, except Ann and Monique, who can bring in the food. I will tend to the wine. We are having a Loibner Riesling Spätlese, gallons of it if you want. I've cooled a case, and I'll pull the corks as long as you will drink it. And then a Tokay Aszu, three *puttonyos*, the best I could get in New York. I've heard those people are trying to bring it back to what it was, in spite of the reactionary taint to it, Father. We'll see."

While Ann and Monique served, he uncorked half a dozen bottles. And then they all began the supper that traditionally was made up of things Grandfather Kerenyi liked: excellent herring, two kinds, one with raw onions and chopped fresh dill in with it, the other with chopped-up preserved beets, and then pâtés, also brought from New York, and cold ham with different kinds of mustard, cold beef and veal, too, and potato salad put together with some unusual ingredients—cut-up cucumbers, for one— the way he liked it, and good brown breads with sweet butter, all of this further garnished with various pickles and relishes, and of course accompanied by the pretty, flowery wine of Austria. They had many, many things to talk to each other about, brother to sister, and so on—and as none of the family was exactly taciturn, not even young Franz at a time like this, there was a great babble for so few voices. Hugo set out to quiz Jeanette, question after question, relentlessly, as was sometimes his method when he wanted to be exceptionally attentive to someone; about her own family in Ithaca, about how they celebrated Christmas and the New Year and birthdays and Memorial and Labor Day, and the Fourth of July, and Easter, if they did, and Thanksgiving; nothing was left out. It rather crushed her with its sheer scope, and embarrassed her, too, because she couldn't really remember that they'd ever done anything in particular, just eaten turkey or roast beef, usually. Then the talk got general around the whole table, voices raised competing for attention, and Aunt Dorcas was at last prevailed upon to lead a recitation of Latin declensions and conjugations, which the family joined in on—*hic haec hoc* and *amo amas amat*—getting mixed up when, prodded by Hugo, they tried to go faster and faster, and finally laughing so they couldn't go on at all, just about the time they got to the subjunctive; and then having a go at *Gallia est omnis divisa in partes tres, quarum unam incolunt Belgae . . .* and so forth, until they couldn't go any further with that, either, and Aunt Dorcas found herself reciting alone, and stopped and said, when Hugo jumped to the buffet for a new bottle of wine to fill her glass, "I fear the Greeks, though they bring gifts," and giggled. She was tipsy. Miriam took some part in the general family fun, though not as she would have in the old days when, if she was in that mood, she'd have led it as much as or more than Hugo; and she talked willingly enough to Grandfather Kerenyi, and did join in toward the end of the Latin recitation, which she continued longer than anyone but Aunt Dorcas. She ate, and she drank wine, but hardly out of gaiety; yet so far, to those who were observing her covertly, nothing seemed too unusual.

Young Franz, sitting beside her, drank a great deal more of the wine. Too much, as particularly Jeanette marked, for the streak of roughness he obviously inherited from his father was intensified by alcohol, and she didn't like it. He came out with things he oughtn't to have, bitingly and in front of people; it verged on physical force. Sure enough, toward dessert—a pastry made up of half a dozen thin layers of cake with filling in between and a buttery, coffee-flavored icing, and candied chestnuts in a silver bowl, and all the rest of the indigestible things these people liked— he suddenly spoke to his mother in his bad way. Much loud talk was going on at Hugo's end of the table, but people like Jeanette learn to hear one certain voice through many others.

"Mother, what made you say that embarrassing thing?"

"What are you talking about now?" Miriam turned toward him so quickly, herself alerted by his tone of voice, that her red shawl fell from her shoulders, revealing to him again just how thin she was, and she had to pull it back up with her right hand.

"About Nicky. About taking his picture. What a time— Christmas Eve—to bring that up! It was morbid."

"Did you find it so? I didn't mean it to be, and don't think it was."

"I hope Ann's kids are too young to understand. Are you going to have a stocking hung on the mantelpiece for him too?"

Miriam replied, "There is this to be said for ghosts, that they are well mannered, and never get intoxicated unless one does oneself. Now stop being censorious, Franzie," she said sharply. "At home, in your own house, all right. But here, in this house, no. One tyrant to a hearth is quite enough."

Franz was a harsh, awkward man, who yet had sensibilities, insights he really didn't want—an uneasy situation at best—and he veered away before his mother's rebuke, less because he thought it deserved than because (his relative sobriety, as yet, apart) he had such uneasy feelings about this whole holiday gathering, and did not want, by poking too long at one hole, to nudge some sullen thing into birth. He had a hard, quick laugh, which he now sounded—a sad thing to hear—poured more Loibner into his high-stemmed glass, drank it off, and then, as he helped himself to Tokay, said around his mother, taking old Mr. Kerenyi's attention from Ann, "Grandfather, tell us about Tokay. Tell us what real Tokay tasted like before the Communists. How this is different."

Grandfather Kerenyi demurred. Surely they didn't want

to hear. Did they? He looked around the table. All of them? It was only fair after so much Caesar, Aunt Dorcas said, intending to be gracious. His austere, old-fashioned stiffness and faintly bitter reserve had been softened by wine and the occasion. "Perhaps, then, I should tell you— for the sake of the record, as they say now."

The old man tried to describe the singularity of classic Tokay, the result of a combination of things—fragrance, golden color, and honeyed sweetness—and history, too; told of the certain life that went with its elegance and style, though he knew all that was suspect and sentimental and had been vulgarized by inappropriate arrangements of Johann Strauss, and of course was all quite antiegalitarian. But . . . He shrugged. Then he described how the grapes were harvested, along the warm southerly slopes of the Hegyalja mountains, how the ones that had aged in the sun, shriveled until their juice was concentrated into an essence, were put into special baskets called *puttonyos*, to be mixed with more ordinary pressings later, and the wine graded accordingly. He demonstrated this from the label of the bottles they were drinking. Once he started, he didn't stop with Tokay, but went on to the other wines of Hungary—from Lake Balaton and Eger—told how once upon a time peasants in native costume danced at the harvest festival, while great magnates with ribbons on their canes and huge hounds, their ladies with parasols and lap dogs, watched and applauded; how the juice was pressed and fermented, with the Church obediently in prayer over it; how the lightest was drunk then, and the better kept in good oak casks (from the Balkan provinces before 1914) and finally bottled to be aged more and more, in cellars dug out under the white castles of the nobility, or below the monasteries whose chapels were capped with golden domes in the shape of onions, or beneath the palaces of the bishops—all those who by the laws of Maria-Theresa paid no taxes on the production of their wines; how these were the wines, Tokay and all, in which the Magyar aristocracy,

the Esterházy, the Kemeny, the Bornemissza, the Gosz-
tonyi, toasted their King, who was, of course, to everybody
else in Central Europe, the Emperor.

And then he began to talk about Budapest and Vienna,
as he almost never did, lest people think him homesick
now that he was old, and be sorry for him. He had come
from a family of Hungarians almost completely Ger-
manized, with their business in Austria and down into the
South Tyrol, and so he had a double nostalgia, for the
Hungary whence his ancestors had come, and for the
Vienna he himself had lived in until 1907, when the business took him to America, where Hugo was born a year
later. Delighted, for it *was* so rare that he talked thus, the
family listened while he described things like the appearances of the old Emperor, who loved the wine of Loiben
they had been drinking earlier: the Emperor in his car-
riage in the streets, in the Imperial box at the opera, waving from his private train, bowing from the balcony of the
Hofburg, uncovering as he arrived at St. Stephen's.

"He was, of course, a very stupid man. There had not
been an intelligent Hapsburg since Maximilian, or anyway since the eighteenth century, Joseph the Second, I
suppose, if you want to grant intelligence to such an eccentric. Even of their line Franz-Josef was outstandingly
stupid, I think, but decorous. Imposing. The lip wasn't so
pronounced in him as it had been in the degenerate Span-
ish branch, for instance, and he was tall and dignified,
which in a monarch is not such a bad substitute for intelligence. He looked, at least, what he was."

"That's surely enough," Hugo said. "An emperor, like a
beautiful woman, can easily be overqualified."

Young Franz, grandson and namesake, entering in, said,
"Right! I married my beloved because she is both beautiful and dumb."

"That is not at all my impression," his grandfather said
coldly.

Franz turned red in the face. With two parents, both, as

he saw them, such wits, ponderous in Hugo's case, perhaps, but with a heavy grace, why was it that his own efforts at repartee so often turned out lumpish? It made him angry at his mother and father. Why hadn't he been taught? He scowled until he saw Hugo put his huge hand over Jeanette's, lift it, and kiss it. Franz laughed again. Jeanette wouldn't be liking that. That wasn't how they showed sympathy in upstate New York. But anyway, not intending to, he had hurt her feelings, and something was called for from him, too.

"That didn't come out the way I meant it," he said. "I meant it to be a compliment." And he got up, pushed back his chair, hesitated over what to do with his napkin, decided to toss it onto the table rather grandly, and went all the way around to his pretty wife; and he, too, kissed her, only on the forehead.

"Bravo, bravo," cried Hugo.

Franz returned to his seat, his mood up. It wasn't so hard. All it took was nerve. A flamboyant gesture. A man could cut a figure after all.

Old Franz resumed the thread of his thoughts, leading him backward. "I never expected to die as old as the Emperor—he was eighty-six, like me, and in fact I've outlived him by a month or two—and I always thought to die closer to him, to go back in the end to be buried in his realm, in the realm he was the last of so many of his house to rule," he said. "As my father was, who did not want to be sent to Hungary for burial. He lies near Klagenfurt. I, on the other hand, will be a long way from Kaiser Franz."

Miriam said, "But next to me. Surely that's better."

Hugo had been kept quiet a long time, and he leapt onto this new subject willingly. "Shouldn't he be next to me?" he asked amusingly. "I mean, I don't think this is at all appropriate for the occasion, but since it's come up, we may as well straighten it out. Our plot, children, has four places in it, and Nicky is already in the second from the left, because your mother didn't want him all by himself on the edge"—he made a face—"so I must either be separated from my wife or my father or both. Unless we were to move Nicky."

Miriam replied, "Nicky must be on one side of me, and if I can get my way, I would like Grandfather on the other. For," she said, turning to the old man, "you have been a person I have loved almost without reservation."

Grandfather Kerenyi stood. "To that, there is no reply possible but a toast. To my beloved daughter-in-law, your wife, your mother, your sister, your grandmother," he said, his glass raised high.

Everyone else at the table stood and drank to Miriam. Even the little children, who'd been given splashes in glasses of their own, stood.

Miriam looked deliberately around, from her son to Monique, Bruce, her sister and her husband, Jeanette, Ann, then back to old Mr. Kerenyi. He waited, looking down at her, never lowering his glass, which shook with the trembling of his hand.

"I must?" she asked him.

"You must," he replied.

Slowly, she stood herself, but did not speak immediately. Again she looked around at everybody. Then, at last, she pulled the flame-colored shawl closer over her shoulders and held it so with her left hand, and in her right raised her own glass.

She said, "I drink to all of you in return. My grandchildren—to eventful lives and some happiness. Franz and Jeanette, to more books and more babies. Ann and Bruce, to the rewards of the world and an enduring capacity to believe in the illusion, if it is one, of their value. Dorcas, to the Baxters, living and dead. Monique, to Scheherazade and suspended solutions. Grandfather, to you above all, to you and all the gallantry that is fading from the earth. And finally Hugo, to your quite correct notion, when you were negotiating this occasion, that it would be unique; so then to all unique occasions, last chances, to circumstances that cannot be reproduced, times that cannot be recaptured, and to final words, of which these are mine."

She swung her glass in a full circle and drank from it.

Obviously with that the evening had passed its climax. Moreover, it was nearly eleven-thirty, and the Cuttler children were drooping. Ann caught her father's attention and said to him, "I have to raise a point about Hugo's Law."

Everybody at the table laughed, and Hugo replied, "What is it? What is it? I am prepared to adjudicate."

"Hugo's Law says, or at least it used to, that children exist for the convenience of adults and not vice versa, and that if they are at table with adults they must act like them."

"Yes, yes. Quite right. And?"

"I have to say that one of mine is going to fall off her chair if we don't move soon."

"Petition granted under terms of the amending article to the Code which says that Hugo can change anything he wants to any time he wants to do so. We will leave the table now, if everybody has eaten enough. Bring wine with you if you want it, and there is cognac, and I will just get the Wilhelmine out of the refrigerator for Father and me and anybody else who wants it. Then we must hang up the stockings. And then the fourth generation can go to bed."

Hugo hurried unnecessarily, as was his way—walking like a man who's missed a train was once Miriam's description—out to the bar refrigerator in the pantry to get a bottle, which he brought into the living room following behind his family. He poured measures of the clear colorless *eau de vie* it contained into stemmed glasses with tiny, cone-shaped bowls, for himself and old Franz, and, as it turned out, for Miriam and Monique, too, while the others took regular brandy—except Jeanette, who, defiantly, had crème de menthe. Hugo sniffed and then tasted.

"Isn't *that* good! Just right. Freezing cold and fiery hot, and smelling the way a pear orchard ought to smell. Isn't that good, Father?"

The old man nodded, immensely pleased. "Very, very. It strikes me that to the qualities you mention should be added another. It feigns, but does not truly possess, freshness and vigor. Instead it has had bouquet bred into it, which is a quality that comes from experience, not youth, a quality belonging in general to those things which are remote from their beginnings, yet have not lost the memory of them. In short, like me," he concluded, "just like me," pointing a finger toward his chest, showing it was a joke.

"Oh, hear that. Hear that, Bruce and Jeanette. Hear him play with us now, the old master. Now you see where I get my taste for exaggerations and phrasemaking. If those are the things Hungarian gentlemen said about alcohols and themselves, just imagine what they found to say about love and ladies and honor and God, eh? But now we must get down to our business."

Hugo got a hammer and three nails and took them to the hearth. Then he felt around with both hands under the wooden mantel, supported by scalloped brackets above the black brick fireplace, searching for old holes that had once been there; but they had been filled in and touched up with stain, he said (although only after he had got a flashlight to look), and he couldn't find them at all. "Damn the unco-operative inanimate—if you don't mind my sounding like a chemistry professor whose demonstration has just blown up. I should have told the painters to leave the old nails in, but I didn't think to. I never thought to have all of you here, or anyway to have the same number of grandchildren, just three, as we once had children in the house, I suppose." He put down his flashlight and looked suddenly around, without getting up, still on all fours. "Just three, the last time they were ever used."

Young Franz, who was standing at a little distance, turned and walked away. He did not want to watch any longer, or to hear anything more; and so while Hugo was hammering new nails into new holes, he sought out his mother, who was down near the Christmas tree, sitting on the window seat sipping her Wilhelmine and fingering the needles on the tips of the boughs.

"Nicky seems to be more than usual on people's minds," he said, his voice subdued. "I wonder why that has to be."

"One thinks of children at Christmas, Franz," she replied. "It's nothing more than that."

"I'm sorry I said that about him to you at dinner." Franz was beginning to feel soft and blurry from all the whisky and wine and now his brandy. "Poor little guy."

"I didn't pay any attention, Franz. You were jealous of Nicky as a boy, you know."

"And why not?"

"Yes, it would have been odd if you hadn't been." She smiled at him. "But it seems to have stayed with you, and that seems too bad."

"So much for my apologizing," Franz said angrily.

Not even when he was very small had his mother forgiven easily. It had been a burden to a boy who had often acted wrongly. "To hell with Nicky," he said, but so that Miriam didn't hear, and then he went to his wife, who was watching this latest Kerenyi Christmas ceremony, who had in fact been chosen to hand Hugo the nails one by one. Franz squeezed her arm to get her attention and murmured into her ear, "Are you beginning to see what it was like to have grown up in this house?" and left her for the brandy bottle back on the silver tray.

When all the nails were in and tested and found firm, Hugo got three old cotton stockings out of a paper bag that had been stuffed in the box with the extra tinsel and

Christmas tree ornaments in the back hall closet, and attached them to the nails. They looked long, huge and delightful to the eyes of the Cuttler children, particularly when cards had been pinned to each one of them with the names Lucy, William, and Victoria written on them. Hugo then made a complicated labor of scattering the coals so that the fire would be entirely burned out by the time of Santa's descent through the chimney. "There. How's that? Wait a minute—I think that little nut of an ember ought to be mashed down. Take the poker and do it yourself, Billy." He whispered an aside to Ann. "Does he still believe in Santa?" She said yes, but teetering. "Good enough, Billy," Hugo said aloud. "And just push these here over to the edge, too. So. How does it look to you? Safe? It's late, so there won't be too much time before he arrives. And now I'll just spread these andirons apart so the old fellow won't hurt a foot, in case he's in a hurry and comes down fast, and you have to remember that because of the narrowness of chimneys, even old ones like this, he has to land with his feet close together, like jumping into a lake from a diving board. Some people claim—did you know this, Lucy?—that he can make himself long and skinny like a worm, so he can get down pipes, I mean stovepipes, if he has to; I don't know myself, never having lived in a place where that was the only way in. There. Now back goes the screen. Don't worry, he'll know how to push that away. How wonderful their faces are, Ann. How I wish that there was something, anything at all, that could so make me fill up with anticipation that I might contain just a quarter of Billy's shining life right now."

Far beyond the children's bedtime though it was, they still had to be allowed their special moment, long rehearsed. Ann had taught them carols, and she now took them to the rear of the living room so that she could sit at the piano and accompany them. Her face was alight with an almost dangerous pride as they did "O Little Town of Bethlehem" and "O Come All Ye Faithful." Then they did the latter a second time, and not too badly, stumbling and having to be prompted only a little, using the words *"adeste fideles."* "I had them learn that for you, Aunt Dorcas," Ann said. The concert closed with "Away in a Manger" and finally "Silent Night," unaccompanied, Ann standing with one arm around each of her children, and everyone else being very solemn at the end, not wanting to be the first to speak.

Until, that is, Hugo said, "Beautiful. Beautiful, dear Ann. You recall, Aunt Dorcas, that just so our own little birds were once taught to sing on Christmas Eve, and you instructed them in *'Adeste Fideles.'* Ann is carrying everything on. Everything that is said about the modern world—we Kerenyis are immune to those disorders, are we not? Here, in this house tonight, there is visible the link between past and present. We have witnessed an epiphany of continuity. Whatever disappears is as surely replaced by something akin."

"Should I, as the patriarch—to use your word—be consoled by that?" Mr. Kerenyi asked.

"The imitation of one generation by another is an immortality, Father, and a profound obedience. There's nothing wrong with that for a consolation."

"Nothing at all."

Hugo clasped Ann's hands, obviously more moved than the occasion really seemed to call for, or than was at all characteristic of him, who was more an ironic or humorous than a sentimental man. "How you have touched me," he said. "And what is more, I must add an observation. We have all spoken of Jeanette's beauty, and quite rightly, but you, too, must receive your lauds. For our daughter is a beauty, too. Different, but still a beautiful woman. You know, when you were playing for the children just now, I thought to myself that with your heavy cheekbones and rather Tartar eyes—gray, slanting, aren't they?—and that wide, stubborn jaw of yours, fit for softening hides, you looked like a medieval Hungarian woman, or a woman of the pagan hordes, strong and enduring like one of them, like a nomad Hungarian woman, but one whose face was reflected in a silver mirror. Do you see? Now how is that for a nicely turned compliment? Our Ann, Miriam, has the face of a Hungarian peasant woman, only seen in a silver mirror."

But Miriam didn't hear and did not reply. She was still seated on the window seat beside the tree, but she seemed to have fallen into a kind of trance, a profound daydream.

"Now really," Hugo said. He went toward her, underlining her inattention to everybody. "Miriam. *Miriam!* Huh. I hope you heard the carols, at least."

She started. "What? Yes. Are they over now?"

"Like the photography," Ann said.

Hugo could organize even an ending. "It's time we broke up. The children must go to bed; Ann has said so. So must Father. Father, I'll carry your suitcase into the back room. No stairs, and you've got your own bath back there, and I warned Mrs. Vendredy to change at home before she comes to cook dinner for us tomorrow. If the rest of you will please carry things out and put them in the dishwasher . . ."

In a few minutes the living room and the dining room were cleared and in some kind of order, and shortly after that everyone had disappeared except Hugo and Aunt Dorcas, who had to stay up and stuff the stockings. They were joined a little later by Ann, and the three of them then put the small toys Hugo had bought at the dime store, and also candy, fruit, and such other trifles, into the stockings hanging at the fireplace. When they had finished, Ann stood off and looked at them, misshapen and lumpy, and smiled.

"They *are* wonderful," she said. "I could wish there were a fourth for me."

"My stockings from years ago. I recognize them," said Aunt Dorcas. "Knit at a mill in Greenfield."

"Miriam's were too fragile. We had to depend on Aunt

Dorcas," Hugo said. "Dorcas provided the stockings and we provided the children."

He began to turn out lights, letting Aunt Dorcas go ahead up to her room, so that he could whisper a moment to Ann in the downstairs hall.

"Well? What do you think?"

"I don't know."

"Do you want to go back into my study and talk?"

Ann shook her head. "Not yet. Offhand, I think it could be worse. I can still hope you exaggerate about it." Ann smiled at him. "That's to be expected; but Grandfather seems to agree with you, and nobody could question his motives."

"Just what do you mean by that?"

"Shhh. I meant, he's not as wrapped up in things here as you are."

"How should I not be? Try to help, Annie. You and Franz. Unless you and Christmas can work a miracle—and I hope you can, I hope you can—I just don't know what will happen to us here in this house. You'll see. You'll see, Ann."

They climbed the stairs, he to his own bedroom on the second floor, next to Aunt Dorcas, Ann to hers on the third. Only the tree was left on, to burn all night in the dark house and remind any late passer-by of Christ's Nativity, if he chanced to make the association.

# two

# conversations

They were whispering downstairs in the hall.

Dorcas heard them as she crossed the hall upstairs, but she couldn't stop then and risk having a humiliating interval before she closed the bedroom door. She listened, though, once it was closed, her ear to the crack, feeling ashamed, but prickly and justified, too. It might be a help in some way to know what people were wanting to whisper about, with the atmosphere in this house so strange tonight and the things Hugo had hinted at over the telephone about Miriam, and with Miriam—yes, it was true; that toast, for instance—behaving . . . behaving . . . so . . . She couldn't catch a single word with her door closed. The one thing certain was that they'd got rid of her. Hugo got rid of her first; then they could whisper.

Well, it stopped. They'd said whatever it was she wasn't meant to know about. Almost certainly it was about Miriam and not about her. There was that.

She heard Ann come up and go on to the third floor, and then Hugo came up too and went into his own room, behind Aunt Dorcas's, opened and closed a closet door, went out into the hall and into the bathroom she shared with him, came back, got into bed (squeakings), and very soon after that began to snore. Loudly and coarsely.

Dorcas didn't even have to undress and settle down and draw up blanket and sheet and even them off to know one thing: she was in for it.

She lay in bed, her hands clasped together as in supplication, staring at a forty-five-degree angle toward the intersection of wall and ceiling opposite her, trying not to hear Hugo now. It was going to be one of those nights when she did not sleep, or slept only so badly that it did her no good at all, when the in-and-out, out-and-in, from fitful dreams to fitful waking and back, was itself an exhaustion. That was the worst of her insomnia: she had to work so hard at it.

Yet she did go to sleep, surprisingly and wrongly. It couldn't last. She came awake, some sound from within or without making her apprehensive, knew that she'd slept, hoped it had been hours but knew it hadn't, and looked at her traveling clock: 1:47. It had only been minutes. A sound . . . Was somebody up? She listened. Nothing but silence. Hugo must have turned over, his legs thrashing like an old bull's. Everyone was asleep, getting rested for the next long day, except poor Aunt Dorcas. In this house filled with people, all of them her family, more or less, Dorcas felt overwhelmingly forlorn. More than anywhere else, here, tangled in this skein of kinships, she felt an outsider. It wasn't her fault. She did her best to be Aunt Dorcas. Whose? Hugo's? Only incidentally. It was Miriam's fault. By her very nature she excluded, and always had, all that was plain and plainly virtuous.

That wasn't fair. There was more to it than that. Too much to think about, but you shouldn't blame *a* person for a whole bushel of causes. Dorcas got up and opened her window a little wider to the bitter night air; sleep cool, her mother always said, and cover up warm. It was too hot in this house—and she hated it, too. For its lack of white woodwork and dentils and a fanlight over the front door; for its disorderly plan and its pretentious leaded windows, and for all the times she had been made uncomfortable in it. Back to bed for another try at sleep. And more sleep. And then waking up again.

Was someone in the hall? Dorcas held her breath. It wasn't her imagination. The sound was so matter-of-fact. Compared with imagined sounds, imaginary voices, it was so unmagical. Someone was going downstairs, someone who surely hadn't come from the third floor or she'd have heard, or from the back of the second floor where young Franz was staying, because that, too, she would have heard; and from Hugo's room there came a rattle as he turned over again, everything flopping. It had to be Miriam. Miriam was going downstairs.

There was no reason why she should not do so; nevertheless, Dorcas tracked her, as if she'd been an intruder, listening, measuring, wondering. And then there came to her a sudden quite strong pulse of feeling. She wanted to join her. She wanted to be with her sister.

Dorcas arose, put on her deerskin slippers and the flannel bathrobe that was fluttering from a hanger near the window, folded her bedclothes back to air and freshen, tiptoed to the door, mindful of Hugo, opened it silently, and started down. The house was in darkness; Miriam was moving through a house dark except for a watery splotch of light that reached the walls of the hallway and the stairwell from the Christmas tree out there in the far corner of the living room. The stairs warned Miriam that someone was coming, but that was all right; Dorcas wasn't trying to surprise her.

Miriam was waiting down near the tree, facing the doorway, when Dorcas got to the ground floor. She held a piece of paper in one hand, that hand, the paper, her face too, all sickly from the blue-green lights beside her.

"Oh, Dorcas, it's you," she said in a very low voice. "What a relief."

Miriam still wore that red thing (dirty purplish now)

over her shoulders. Dorcas, scandalized, blurted out, "Why, you've never even gone to bed. What's the matter with you?"

"What are you doing up?"

"I've had insomnia. Sleeping in a strange bed. And too much of that perfumy wine with supper, I think. Hazel says it affects your whole metabolism." Dorcas added, embarrassed, "Of course it was good. Everything was good. Just too much of it."

Miriam smiled. "Yes, too much—if it was sleep you were really after, Dorcas," she said. She turned around. "Am I wrong not to like the idea of these lights burning all by themselves? Hugo would say I am indulging myself in a death wish, or some such silly phrase. He pelts me with those words, and tries to get my doctors to. Finding shaming new names for respectable old states of mind. Would you ever have imagined that Hugo would take to vulgarized psychology, like everyone else? I would have thought he'd never do that, at least that the sense of Voltaire laughing at him from the shadows would have stopped him. He wouldn't let Ann and Franz in the house tonight until he'd lit it all up first. I heard him running around and I'm sure that was what he was doing. Leaving lights on is just another of those hollow things people do now—the way they kiss near strangers and use their first names. It pretends to be friendly, but it cheapens real intimacy. So . . ." She stopped.

Dorcas said, "We still call the girls in our oldest forms Miss So-and-so, but it's under fire."

"And then, in this case, I don't think it's safe. There could easily be a short circuit." So suddenly that Dorcas gasped, Miriam jerked off her scarf and whipped it up into the air with her free hand, then around and around like a banner in a high wind. "It would go like that," she said. "And the whole house with it. A conflagration, while we slept. Me. You. Babes in arms. The whole house flames and sparks and ashes. The whole house."

Dorcas agreed. "Yes, just like that. There are stories in the newspapers every year. More often because of candles, but short circuits too. And it's a waste of electricity."

"You sound like Mother now," Miriam said. "We never think about saving anything—electricity or anything else."

"I don't like that. Waste is waste; Mother was right."

Miriam put her shawl back on over her shoulders. "It's never mattered, because of Grandfather Kerenyi," she said indifferently.

"Extravagance is wrong for its own sake."

"Dorcas, tell me something. Did you ever like coming here? Did you ever want to be with us during your vacations or at times like this?"

Dorcas didn't say anything.

"You've stopped for several years now, but I wondered about earlier," Miriam said.

Dorcas replied, "Well, you're not Hazel's family. I don't like leaving her all alone, and she doesn't seem to think she fits in."

"Did you really want to come this time?"

"I didn't want to, no."

"Why did you come, then?"

"When Hugo told me that everybody would be here, I didn't exactly want to miss it, either. You're all I've got left."

Miriam said, "And of course he got at your conscience, because of me, didn't he?"

"Yes, he did, or he tried to. He said you were in such a bad frame of mind that everyone had to help. Including me. I'll be honest. Even so, I tried to get out of it. But he said I owed it to you and him—and to our mother and father. To their memory. That it was that serious."

"Your poor, overused New England conscience. You don't need to tell me more."

"A person can refuse only so long, and Hazel thought I'd better come and said she would, too. For tomorrow."

"I know." Miriam squatted down, put her hand behind the felt that draped the stub of the tree, found the main plug where Hugo had tucked it after he first turned on the lights, and pulled it out, so that the room went all dark. There was enough light, once one's eyes got used to it, to give a hint of the shapes of things, but a capricious light, touching only here and there—a place on the wall or the ceiling, a back of a chair. Miriam stood up, and it brightened one of her shoulders and one of her eyes—one only—caught the white so that it gleamed uncannily at Dorcas. It was only the way the streetlight nearest the house worked in here, but it went with talking to Miriam. Miriam approached. She took Dorcas by the hand and led her to the couch close to the dead fire.

"Hugo wanted to make the family past powerful this holiday," she said, sitting down, pulling Dorcas down to sit opposite her. "Or so he has been saying. He never realizes how dangerous some of his ideas are. It's what comes of assuming that all—" She hesitated, searching. "That all filiations lead toward oneself, never away." She smiled. "Did you notice, for instance, how we almost lost old Franz to the past tonight? One push at the right moment, I thought, and he might have gone forever. I've been thinking myself, since I went up to my room, about things like the house on West Hadley Avenue. Don't you, Dorcas? Think about it? Don't you find West Hadley Avenue coming back to you during your insomnia? Truer than in dreams? With Mother's blue iris all in bloom down the east border between us and the Cunninghams?"

Sitting in a dark room, in a house full of sleeping people, at three in the morning, talking about the house of one's girlhood, was not what Dorcas could approve of for Christmas Eve. She resisted. "It was torn down twenty years ago," she said.

"That doesn't matter."

"To put up an A and P. Doesn't that?"

"Think of the iris, smelling like Concord grapes."

In spite of her disapproval, Dorcas said softly, *"Gallia est omnis divisa in partes tres . . ."*

"Exactly. That rather touched me tonight. I wished I'd studied harder and memorized more so I could have gone on and on with you."

*"O saepe mecum tempus in ultimum . . ."*

"What is that?"

"Horace. One of the Odes. He gave them to me before I went away to Wellesley, just the night before, at dinner. I can't teach Horace. He's too racy. That one ends all about getting drunk. That'll all change, as things are going. I, for one, look forward to it."

Miriam smiled. "Mary will read Horace, but Miss Smith can't. I was envious of you, getting those books each birthday and Christmas."

"The Loeb Classics have never been improved on."

"Envious because you were so good at it, and he was so proud of you for that."

"Yes, he was proud of my Latin and Greek. But he got much delight from you."

"How nicely you put it. He got delight from me. I think he did."

They sat a bit, both looking toward the fireplace where the coals were now completely dead, just from habit. It was not so warm any more. Dorcas adjusted her bathrobe.

"Sometimes," she said slowly, "I was afraid he loved you more than he did me, no matter how hard I parsed my verbs."

"What a thing to say! To have thought about, I mean. Why do we have to compare our places in people's hearts?"

"It's natural. There were just the two of us, and I had a right to half. I wanted my fair share."

"But Dorcas, how in the world would you measure out a fair share of our father's affections? As far as that goes, who in the world, in talking of an equal division of love, would ever really mean half?"

"I did."

"Well, anyway, you didn't need to worry."

"No, you're right. You were pretty and quick and amusing, and I was intelligent and industrious. We balanced. I always came back to that. We balanced. He didn't love you more."

"Could you ever have forgiven such an injustice, Dorcas?"

"I would have become reconciled to it."

"He has to have been the most kind and gentle man that ever there was."

"And fair."

"Dorcas, what a nice piece of baggage that feeling is, for us to have had to carry out of our childhood. Baggage, baggage. I'm busy these days ridding myself of it—as one must in the end."

"Why should you do that?" Dorcas said firmly. "There's nothing wrong with you, Sister."

"I didn't say there was. But it takes a long time to get rid of unnecessary baggage. As long as it takes to collect it, and that's why I've already started. It's a sore point in this house. Hugo loves all baggage, the more the better. We're at war, Hugo and I, over baggage."

"From what you were just saying—about iris and all—it sounds to me as if you're doing anything but getting rid of baggage, as you put it."

Miriam answered seriously. "No, you're wrong about that. I am going through memories as one rereads old letters before burning them. One must take both out, handle them, think about them, in order to break their hold."

"War. Baggage. Burning memories as one burns letters. You're just being dramatic. You've always had that weakness."

"How censorious you are too, Dorcas—the same streak Franz has in him. It certainly isn't a Kerenyi quality, so he must have it from me, but it wasn't a Baxter quality either. It's a Tewkes trait; Mother had it, you do, and now Franz."

"It's not being censorious to tell you to keep your feet on the ground."

Miriam's whisper became touched with impatience. "Simple things said in an artful way may still be true." She started to get up, but changed her mind. "Dorcas, we never talk any more. Let's stay up a while longer and talk about the things we remember. Let's say a catalogue of them. Like Aunt Min's farmhouse at Hockley Center, and sugaring off. The sweet new sap cooked down and dribbled into a fistful of packed snow. Eating it like toffee, so sweet it hurt your mouth. And then the pickle, to clear it out."

Dorcas said grudgingly, almost forgetting to whisper, "How about the glider on the front veranda at Taggert's Summer Hotel on Mount Aesopus, and Mother scolding when Father made it shimmy to make us giggle."

Miriam said, "Sunday evenings at home. I liked them. I was always so glad that day was over. Church with Mother was over for another week. Supper in the kitchen—gingerbread. It all sounds so conventional, doesn't it?"

"Building wren houses from hemlock slabs."

Miriam said, "I'm still on things to eat. Probably no better than what we get now, but our tongues were younger, isn't that so, Dorcas?" She laughed. "Creamed codfish, and that smell of salt cod when it comes out of the little box. Aunt Min's apples, too. Northern Spies and Jonathans. They were small and had bird pecks and sometimes worms, but they were real apples. And then, I have to say it again: Mother's gingerbread. Baked in that iron thing—or was that something else? Anyway, it doesn't seem possible that I'd have such—have such trouble with the memory of gingerbread. But that gingerbread *was* good, and I really *do* believe that nothing has ever tasted quite the same since. Cheap and good. I hope I'm being down-to-earth enough for you now."

"Hazel makes it, but it isn't as good, and I can't tell her why, although I tell her it isn't."

"So even Hazel doesn't always measure up to Mother."

Dorcas was suddenly on her guard. She said stiffly, "She doesn't try."

Miriam said, "Oh, Dorcas." She took one of Dorcas's hands, an unexpected movement that made Dorcas shrink back, for they were not given to touching each other in the Baxter family. "How comforting to think of summer vacations at Taggert's, and Aunt Min's for a late-winter weekend, and eating Mother's cooking, and reading Latin with Father. And yet, how dangerous—more so than almost anything else I know of."

Dorcas intoned softly, "*Lugete, O Veneres Cupidinesque . . .*"

"What is that, Dorcas?"

"You wouldn't know. You wouldn't ever have seen it. He kept it under lock and key. But that last summer when we took him to Aunt Min's and he couldn't read for himself, he told me where it was and had me bring it along and had me read it to him. Catullus. That was Catullus. I would never read Catullus to another human being, much less another man."

"Catullus. So he had Catullus locked up all those years."

"It upset me very much at first. Not just reading it, but the idea of his liking it. Finally I came to realize that it wasn't that he was—flawed in a way I hadn't known, just that he had other sides to him, not necessarily bad, but not what I'd expected. I guess he sensed some of what was going on in my mind, because one day he said to me that Catullus was the best lyric poet in Latin, and so if we didn't read him because of prudery, it was our loss. I didn't argue, but there are some things no poet is good enough to say—that was my feeling. I suppose he knew it would be, so he hid the book out of consideration for me when we were younger. And Mother."

"Who wouldn't have understood it."

"Couldn't have. No."

They sat quietly. Then Miriam said, "I thought that Ann was going to carry on your side of the family tradition, you know, and go into the Classics."

"She had as much talent as I, certainly. Has she kept the Loebs I used to give her each year?"

"I doubt that there's the right spot for them in the Cuttler house, but perhaps she's put them away somewhere and can take them out later on—if she needs to."

"I was disappointed when she didn't go on."

"Don't feel that."

"He'd have been disappointed, too."

"We make terrible bonds for ourselves when we reproach other people for not doing or being as we wish," Miriam said, not whispering at all. "The worst there are. Impossible to break, almost. I've come to think benevolent indifference the best of all attitudes."

Dorcas said, "Both Father and I looked forward most, that last summer, to Virgil." She started in again: "*Arma virumque cano, Troiae*—" But Miriam interrupted her.

"What did they really think of Hugo, Dorcas, Father and Mother?"

"Mother was sorry he was a foreigner."

"But he wasn't."

"Well, first generation, anyway."

"Is that all?"

Dorcas said, "She disapproved of your living in New York and leading the life you did, and while it's not fair, she thought Hugo went with all that. I don't know that she ever believed he really could have gone to Harvard, so little of it had rubbed off."

"And Father?"

"I don't know. He didn't talk about people much."

"He'd have said so if he liked Hugo. He gave out praise easily enough."

"That's true."

"Tell me what you know. Please, Dorcas. I'm on the trail of a long view, don't you see?"

"Of course he had some reservations about Hugo, as you can imagine." Dorcas was flustered. "But you were bound to marry, and there's no accounting for tastes. Not that. That sounds worse than it was."

"Then how bad was it?"

"He and Mother used to talk about it sometimes before she died. She was always saying she didn't face death as comfortably as she might have because she was uneasy about you."

"We already know that about her. But Father?"

"Father joked whenever Mother talked about dying. He said once that there wasn't a problem eternity wouldn't take care of, including Hugo."

"Eternity, yes."

"Once he said he thought you'd have a houseful of people all the time and that you might get tired of it. That's just a remark he made that comes back to me. It's innocent enough."

"Oh, very."

"You know how he didn't believe in having more than a couple of people around at once."

"Sometimes I've been dazzled. No, it's not been all bad, having the crowds."

"I don't think he thought it would be. Just that it would go on and on. And you can't really talk to a crowd, he thought."

"No, but you can declaim."

"And he said once—it was when you'd come to see him just before he died, you remember, at Aunt Min's. Hugo came up for the weekend and took you away. Somebody, it might even have been me—it must have been, because Min had stopped making any noises at all except that terrible kind of gurgling when she sang—said something to him about how it was nice to have the house quiet again. He said it was always nice to have a house quiet. I guess I went on to say—well, it's the truth, and I said it—to say that Hugo had a loud voice and used it a lot, and Father said—I'm quoting as exactly as I can—'That's Hugo's particular way of having things quiet around him.' I remember because it gave me food for thought."

"As well it might."

"And then he said, 'I always knew it was a long way from Northampton to Budapest, but now I know it's just as far from Budapest to Northampton. What I never would have guessed is that my Miriam would have turned out to be such a traveler.' "

The Baxter girls sat quietly for a long time. At length Miriam shook her head. "Poor Hugo. He tried. Not really hard, but he tried. He's always been such a Pied Piper, charming his troupe along behind him—but then, he's always been able to select the troupe. He could never understand his failure with a high-school Latin teacher and a God-fearing baker of gingerbread." After a bit, she added, "It was a bleak thing that Father said about distances, wasn't it?"

"Not all that bleak."

"What he didn't spell out is that from the center of one being to the center of another is infinite, and who ever tries to make that long a journey?"

It sounded too fancy to Dorcas. She said, "People from different backgrounds are bound to be different."

Miriam laughed. "We're a funny pair, you and I. Well, nobody can ever be everything or have everything or keep everything, no traveler can. It's all a question of losses, isn't it, Dorcas, right from the beginning, losses and deprivations, and then gains and endowments. I'm sententious tonight, I'll say that."

Dorcas said, "You like the sound of words too much. I think you like the sounds more than their meanings. It's more important to you for the things you say sometimes to sound well than for them to be true."

"What an idea. Well, we'd better go to bed and try to sleep a while. Come on."

Miriam got up and led the way through the dark house

to the stairs. She was almost to the landing, Dorcas stepping carefully behind her, not being so familiar with them, when she stopped. "Lord, I forgot what I really came down for." She waved the paper she'd been holding in her hand, which Dorcas, while they talked, had identified as an envelope. "It's about tomorrow. It's a note for Hugo, for him to get first thing in the morning. I'll put it on the mantel above the stockings where he's sure to see it." She did so, and on her way back stooped down and relighted the tree. "It's not mine to turn off," she remarked, upon rejoining her sister.

Together they climbed to the upstairs hall and there separated.

Hugo was the first person up on Christmas morning, lumbering around his bedroom, thumping and squeaking, clearing his throat and blowing his nose, flushing the toilet twice: Dorcas heard it all. He had to be, because it had been arranged that he would not only provide the little presents from Santa Claus that had already been stuffed into the children's stockings, but also Santa's big ones, which would lie, or stand in the case of Billy's new bicycle, beside the tree. He might have brought them out the night before but hadn't wanted to; he didn't trust children not to sneak down and peek; it had been known to happen in this very house. And so he had to get downstairs before anybody else did and take them to the living room, depending on Ann to keep her children on the third floor until he called up for the whole family to assemble. Nor did he, as he moved around, look toward the top of the mantel where Miriam's note sat.

In accordance with a Kerenyi tradition of Hugo's invention, everybody would enter the living room in a special way. They would bunch together in the doorway and look in, and then at last, when the excitement had grown unendurable, they would come in, all together, on the march, while Ann, taking over this time what had always been

Miriam's job, would play a slam-bang version of "Hark the Herald Angels Sing." Everyone had to sing it, too, not just stomp forward with more or less high-lifting knees. Then they could break ranks and run around to see all the presents, glittering and shining, and the stockings hanging fully laden, waiting to be distributed. Only this morning it couldn't be done promptly, because Miriam was late. Someone had heard water running in her bathroom; she was up, but she was late. Everyone else was in the downstairs hall at seven-thirty, even old Mr. Kerenyi, in his heavy quilted dressing gown. The Cuttler children were wildly restless, whining to know how much longer it would be, quite beyond Monique's efforts to keep them diverted or suppressed. Something of their frenzy got communicated to Victoria, who for the first time really began to cry. Jeanette tried to calm her down, and Franz, who wasn't feeling at all well, cursed and walked into the dining room and back in order not just to have to stand still and endure the noise and his own queasiness. Bruce Cuttler watched the scene with some amusement and didn't get involved; it was too much a Kerenyi scene for that. But Ann finally suggested that they at least go on into the living room and wait there instead of this milling around in the hall. And it was then that Dorcas thought to tell Hugo that Miriam had left him a note on the mantel. Hugo asked her how she knew, and Dorcas replied that she'd heard Miriam prowling and had got up and talked to her in the middle of the night.

Hugo gave her a quick look, full of suspicions (or so it seemed to Dorcas), went off, and returned with the note. He opened and read it by the light from the wall sconce.

He looked around—at Ann, at Franz, who couldn't meet his father's eyes, at Dorcas—those who he felt were most involved with his problems with his wife.

"She isn't joining us," he said.

"Not for the stockings?" Ann asked in disbelief.

"For any of it. She isn't coming down. Here, I'll read her

note. It says: 'Hugo—' " He glanced up. "Not 'Dear Hugo,' of course. 'Hugo. I have decided not to join you when you open the presents tomorrow'—it's dated last night, at two a.m.—'but I'll be glad to talk to anyone who wants to come and see me in my sitting room during the morning. M.' And she adds, as a postscript, 'I will not be moved to change my mind by any arguments, so do not bother to try.' "

"Oh, dear," said Dorcas guiltily. "She certainly didn't tell me this. Not come down. Oh, dear."

"That's all?" Ann said. "That's all she says?"

"That's all." Hugo crumpled the note and threw it up the stairs. "Not be moved to change her mind. What . . . arrogance. I think I will go up and make her come down."

"How will you do that?" Bruce Cuttler asked.

"She has broken her pact with me," Hugo answered. "I can use force." He tempered that threat after a quick look at the Cuttler children. "I will bang on her door until she has to come down, knock it open, knock it off its hinges. I will make her prefer coming down to staying."

Old Mr. Kerenyi said quietly, "The time has passed for that."

"With my fists." Hugo waved them in the air.

The baby let out a real howl, frightened now, and little Lucy's face screwed up, ready for tears, as she interpreted this noisy scene as meaning further delay in getting at the Christmas presents. She ran to her daddy. Hugo got to the first step, but Ann had no trouble in catching his sleeve, and then no trouble in holding him back.

She said, "I'll go up. I'll try. Everyone else stay here."

She ran up the stairs, tapped on her mother's sitting-room door, got no answer, and then went toward the back of the hall and around a corner and knocked on the door that led directly into Miriam's bedroom. Again she got no answer at first, and so she said, through the wooden panel, that it was Ann, and if her tap wasn't answered, Hugo would soon be pounding instead.

Miriam came. She unlocked the door and opened it. "So he has my note, then."

"Yes. Let me in a moment."

Miriam stepped back, and in fact retreated to her bedside. She turned on a little light.

Ann said, with a shiver, for it was cold, "Everybody's waiting. The children are wild. Mother, this simply isn't fair. What does it mean?"

"Why, just what I said, Ann. That I'm not going to join you. Is that so unfair? Why should I have to?"

"Why should you? But it's the high point of Christmas— for the children, I mean. It's the whole point."

"I did it many times. I do not want to start in again. That's all. I don't want to join you."

"But it's—it's insulting."

"Not insulting. Maybe something more, maybe less."

"And very hurtful."

"Something more. I'm sorry for that. And I don't want it to be, although it is perhaps not easily got around."

"Mother, you must come down."

"Ann, I won't."

They looked at each other. Finally Ann said, "Father mentioned a pact. What pact?"

"Oh, when he was carrying on about having everyone here, I agreed to show up for things. That's all. He took it as a pact and has been bullying me with it ever since. Whether or not it was, on my part, or simply fatigue, taking the easy way to quiet him down, I'm not sure. Either way, I'm not going to do it this morning. I have reasons."

"A pact like that," Ann said, "that's very strange of both of you."

"Your coming was his idea, and 'pact' was his word. I didn't finally oppose it. Sooner or later, Ann, you would have had to see for yourself. Not Franz, perhaps, but you. Now go along and open your presents and come to me later if you like."

Ann said, "I don't care what you say, I'm both insulted

and hurt. Do you think it was easy to get the children and Bruce here? And I've been looking forward to it, too. After all—well, why should I have to explain why?"

Miriam didn't reply.

Sometimes Ann had her father's quick temper. "This thing you're doing, Mother. It's not dramatic or provocative or ironic or arresting or revealing or anything else that might make an effective anecdote for you later. You're doing something that's plain unforgivable."

Ann went downstairs, where she told the others they would have to go on without Miriam. When her father made an angry gesture and started for the staircase again, she stopped him. They looked at each other; he gave in without further argument, a little to Ann's surprise; a relief, yet a puzzle, too. And so her family entered the living room and opened their presents without Miriam Kerenyi. But it could hardly be said that she was not on everybody's mind, excepting only her grandchildren's.

It was all over by eight-thirty, and after that it was time for breakfast, which was to be light, Hugo said—toast and coffee and orange juice, eggs only on insistence—and which had to be prepared by the ladies and eaten and got over before Mrs. Vendredy came to cook the turkey, which would be about nine-thirty, he thought. In the meantime he and Bruce and Franz would clean up the living room, and burn all the wrapping paper and ribbons and cards that were scattered over the floor. Ann let Jeanette and Monique and Dorcas cook, while she took her children up to see their grandmother, for she couldn't bear to have matters between them left as they had been.

Miriam was still in her bedroom, but was now lying on the bed in a dressing gown, the curtains open, window closed. Billy and Lucy came forward with Miriam's present from the Cuttlers: a stole, a broad and long one of tans and browns and cream-colored alpaca wool, labeled as being made by the Indians of Peru. That done, they were sent away to play with their new things until their breakfast was ready.

Ann sat down on a little bedside chair, pulled around to face her mother.

She said, in her more usual, coolish way, "Do you think I should apologize to you? Perhaps I will want to."

"Apologize for what?"

"For what I said earlier."

"Why should you? You do have a lot to learn. We aren't going to be on apologizing terms with each other any more."

Ann spoke more intensely. "Mother, what in the world is going on? You've really got to tell me."

"The celebration of Christmas, nineteen-sixty-eight."

"You didn't use to be arch."

"Nor you to sound quite so much like—well, like a bright young North Shore matron, squaring away to deal with a problem."

"Is that what I sound like? The problem, anyway, appears to be there, at least. More than I thought at first."

"Yet Hugo must have presented his—or rather let me say *a* case—very fully, not to mention urgently, to have brought about all this hiving. You can't be entirely surprised."

"He was certainly not nonchalant."

Miriam laughed. "What a word for him! Just what was his presentation?"

"Briefly, that if we all came together, as in the old days, only augmented now by husbands and wives and children, it might make a difference. To you. He said it might reverse the direction you are intent on taking."

"Not a very alluring invitation."

"No, but compelling enough. Coupled with the fact that every letter he's written the last ten months, and some of them before that, too, have contained black hints and open complaints that he is unhappy."

"He is managing."

"That you are making him unhappy."

Miriam made a quick gesture of dismissal.

"Well, you asked."

"I tried to explain to him, several times. I've given up. It isn't possible to explain anything to your father that he doesn't already know, particularly if it involves an inconvenience."

"I think you're too hard on him."

Miriam looked at her a long time. "I hope you won't take sides, Annie," she said.

"Take sides over what?" Ann replied quickly.

"Should I talk about it to you? Expound it, I mean. Point one, point two, point three?" Miriam mused. "I had thought I should. Now I'm not so sure. Maybe the example is better, after all, than words. You had one this morning."

"I want words, too."

"And if I talk to you, will you promise to let it scratch through the veneer?"

"I promise to hear it, which is more than you've been granted so far, isn't it?"

"Yes. All right. I'll tell you. It comes out to a small thing. I've changed."

"Oh, is that all?"

"It's so very simple, if only people would just let it be."

"Simple!"

"I know what you mean—what could be more complicated? And in a way you're right. Only complicated isn't the right word—not that you've used it. Radical more than complicated. Like saying the climate has changed. Naturally, if you want to range out in search of smaller consequences—a mouse without a seed one morning, the migrating bird that doesn't stop—you can amass complexities; but the basic idea is simple. The climate changed. Yes." Miriam thought about it. "From hot to cold or wet to dry. That's all. A simple, fundamental change."

"That changes the lives of everything connected with it."

"Anyway, it was only an analogy."

"Just what is the change?"

"Why, I don't like crowds any more."

Ann frowned. "I don't understand."

"It's what your grandfather Baxter once said about Hugo and me. About our life. Crowds. That there would be crowds. I've been thinking about it this morning. He said he thought I'd get tired of having them around. He was right. It took some time, but that is what it's come down to. You ought to understand, because I remember how you dodged my crowds in the days when I was standing in the doorway waving them in off the street. When I fancied myself as a hostess in the tradition of Hugo's century, that it might be said of me someday that at her 'afternoons' were first thought up half the great ideas of modern times. Some such ridiculous thing as that. Yes, how you did run from them. Would you now?"

"I do what I have to do, Mother. But I keep a watch on myself from a suitable distance."

"Thank God for that. I hadn't your detachment, Annie, and perhaps I lack your poise. Meaning it as a virtue. That kind. But anyway, I'm tired of parties and fancied roles, not to mention universities and faculty wives and their husbands, everything to do with careers, and with house-holding; also of going on trips to Europe or anywhere else, of all objective knowledge, so-called, above all of talk, talk, talk, and worrying about other people, including you and Franz and your families. I've got other things I'd rather do."

"Which are?"

Miriam's reply was a long time in coming, and when she made it, she turned her head and looked away from her daughter. "When I am alone, in this room or elsewhere, I am content."

Ann grasped that this might not be just one more Kerenyi crisis, which would finally resolve itself after enough trouble for everybody. Carefully, she said, "Let's talk about hurting people again. You know, Mother, you hurt my feelings when you stopped listening to the Christmas carols last night. You did, didn't you? The children were really singing them for you. Father would have been just as satisfied without them, with only the stocking part, where he gets to use the hammer, or at most some stanzas of 'The Night Before Christmas.' I taught them the carols for you. Because, as he said, you taught them to us. I find I am paying attention to things like that."

Miriam looked back at Ann. "I am realizing—Hugo has accomplished this with his plans—that there are by-products, side effects to my change, that I don't necessarily like. Well, so I've just got to keep my courage—determination?—up."

"You may not want us any more, but we still want you."

"You have to respect what has happened to me."

"Maybe. How long will it last?"

"As long as I do. If another change comes, it won't be to return to what you would probably call normal, Ann. I can promise that."

"I don't quite believe all this. There's something false about it. Posturing is the word that comes to mind. Or maybe your description, your words, don't really convey what you want them to. It sounds so—so away out there, happening to someone else. As if it didn't matter much. A thing one might even take as amusing—serious, to be sure, but faintly amusing."

"That, more or less, is the tone I want."

"Anyway, it doesn't make any sense. People don't change. They stay the same. Circumstances may change, and circumstances may change people, or seem to. Have you some new circumstance, I am wondering."

Miriam replied, "I've got ideas about all that. I'll tell them to you, too. An older woman's wisdom. Some people have the potentiality for becoming different built into them: that's what stays the same, that possibility, in their cases. Climates can change, let's say; therefore changeability is a fixed characteristic of climates. Not of every-thing—or everybody. Hugo doesn't. He's unyielding and monolithic, is Hugo."

"I think he's very miserable, Mother."

"He'll certainly be telling you so—for a while longer."

"And I'll listen. I think you owe him, and us, an effort to pull yourself out of this—what should I call it?—this mood you've gone into."

"I deny that. Everybody—Coral Pinckney, for instance; you'll hear her on the subject, too, I don't doubt—says I should do it because Hugo wants me to and because we've been married a long time and he's unhappy, or because it's what everybody else wants me to do, or because I ought to be happier if only I did. What kinds of reasons are those?"

"Good ones, I'd have said."

"I deny that, too. I will stay the way I am, the way I am now. And perhaps you should be grateful. There are, after all, many other ways I might have gone. Flight. I could have disappeared. And not just out the back door. I've at least chosen to remain visible. Your father hasn't to be left in doubt, or remorse, at least. I make no intolerable mys-tery of my—folding in."

Ann said, "He's got lots of things on his side you can't ignore. I agree with Coral. There's love and habit and a common history of thirty-five years. You can't act as if all that hadn't ever been."

Miriam said flatly, "I shall never again participate in the life of my family as I once did. It will be much better for you if you learn that now, Annie. And there is nothing, nothing in the world, you can do or say, or anyone else, ei-ther, to bring me back. I have changed!"

Ann watched her mother, as if for signs, some necessary clue to make all this comprehensible. "Why, Mother? Why?"

"Well, you see, as I look back over my life, it seems to me to have been made up of a series of what I call to myself 'rites of passage.' Or a series of pulsations, a trajectory with new thrusts given it. Metamorphoses is too strong. I've gone from one state into another, at certain times, beginning in one and ending in another, related, yet each with its own integrity, like parent and child, but more continuous. Do you see what I mean at all, Annie? I really do want you to. Particularly you." She reached out and patted Ann's hand; Ann did not flinch, like Dorcas. "They're obvious enough, mostly. Like going from girlhood into womanhood. That one. What an idea, I still say, to treat it as an advance, a moving forward, an *improvement*. I can still recall things from my childhood so pleasurable that I can hardly bear that they should have been superseded and must finally be discarded. I suppose Dorcas would say I'm being histrionic. False, anyway . . ."

"Not just Dorcas . . ."

"Ah, Annie, I know it's not—Chicago talk."

". . . but not necessarily me."

"Later I went to New York to be liberated, as you know. That, too, was a passage. I left behind me the people and places I still revisit. Marriage. That meant being different, not just being added on to. By Hugo. By you children. All the rest. New. There was Nicky's death. I've wondered about it, but I think that was only a shock to me; it didn't precipitate a change, as I'm speaking of them."

"I'm not so sure."

Miriam said thoughtfully, "I grieved for him a long time, and I still do, to some degree. But how he would complicate my life now, if he were alive. I might not be able to carry out my plans at all. He might give Hugo the weapon he needs. Does that, I wonder, oblige me to be thankful for what happened?"

*"Mother!"*

"Or at least not to regret it? Yet how unkind."

"Mother, this is really very uncomfortable and rather crazy talk. I don't like it. I don't know if I should listen to more of it."

"I'm showing you one way, Annie. You'll have my example."

"I don't want it."

Miriam went on. "And then, of course, there was the change everybody knows about, the second physiological one. That was hard. It was harder than leaving girlhood behind."

"You don't have to tell me. I remember."

"You got married in the middle of it."

"Small wonder."

"And then my illness of last winter—that opened the way to what I am now. What I am becoming. The sheer seduction of not being responsible to anybody for anything, of not caring or having to care, of being placed quite outside the normally expected range of behavior. A prolegomenon to another rite of passage—I saw that point to it. But I was, it turned out, only a catechumen, after all. One could say, I suppose, that I am continuing my studies."

They gazed at one another, the two women. Jeanette called from downstairs that breakfast was ready, and Ann stood up to leave.

"Later," Miriam said, "after you are all through, could someone bring me coffee and a piece of toast? To my sitting room?"                                    •

Ann nodded. She said, "I must think about all this. I'll have to talk to people. To Franz."

"If you like."

"And Bruce."

"I assure you, I don't care."

"I know. I was only giving you fair warning." Ann leaned over and kissed her mother. "How I shall miss you," she said lightly, pretending it was all a kind of joke.

"Oh, it doesn't mean we can't talk now and then, Annie," Miriam replied.

And that was the way they left it.

———

Immediately after breakfast Ann began to prepare a tray
for her mother in the kitchen and was caught at it by Hugo,
who demanded to know what it was for, and was talked out
of forbidding food to go upstairs to his wife, which he
thought he had the right to do in this his own house, only
when Ann argued that if Miriam was challenged that way,
something worse might happen. Hugo knew at once.

"She might not come to dinner."

Ann nodded solemnly.

"That will surely be the end of things," he said.

"It would be sad."

And so the danger was put into the minds of everybody
who was in the kitchen at the time—Aunt Dorcas and
Monique and old Mr. Kerenyi.

Carrying the tray up was to be Monique's duty, by her
meek request. Ann, who thought that Jeanette and Franz
should take their baby in to see Miriam without delay,
went to tell them so. They had left the living room, but she
found them in their own quarters; Jeanette was back in the
nursery room, and Franz was lying on his bed, a forearm
thrown over his eyes.

He refused. "I don't want to go to her now, Annie."

Ann said, "You've got to go sometime soon. And we
have to talk it over."

"Later. I'll send Jeanette now."

"At least that. Keep pressure on Mother. Remind her of
ourselves."

"Is it really serious?"

"Very, I should say. Be careful today. You know what I
mean. Please. We need all our wits."

"What's it all about?"

"Find out, Franzie." Ann then added, a little contemp-
tuously, "You might say that Mother is suffering from a
hangover from her earlier life, I think."

Franz smiled a little. "We Kerenyis do believe in the
power of clever words to illuminate situations, don't we?"
he remarked.

When Franz told Jeanette to take the baby in to see Miriam, she, too, had her questions.

"Why aren't you coming with me?"

"One at a time. Fill up Mother's morning more."

"Why didn't she come out to say hello last night? Why didn't she come down this morning?"

"I don't know."

"Was she just being rude?"

"Whatever she's doing certainly transcends rudeness."

"I call it rude."

"Well, I don't. And I have more reason not to like it than you."

"And that father of yours. I'm not going to drive back to Newark with him tomorrow. We'll have to get there some other way. I don't care how much it costs. I don't mind about my own life, but he's not going to risk Victoria's again." The baby made a noise from Jeanette's arms, pronounced one of her three or four words, and Jeanette cooed back at her. "We don't matter so much," she murmured, "and he certainly doesn't. But she has her life ahead of her."

"Intensity compensates for duration, or so Father would say."

"And what is more, maybe he'll write a book or two and some magazine articles, but she'll have beautiful, wiggly little babies," Jeanette said, in baby talk.

"There would seem to be a need for each."

Seeing that he was not up to a real fight, Jeanette went ahead. "My father may be only a telephone-company engineer in upstate New York and not a Princeton professor, but at least he never tries to browbeat my mother or the rest of us."

"It will all be over in twenty-four hours," Franz said, sighing. "Now be nice and go along with Victoria, the way Ann said to. The faster we get on with all this, the faster it will seem possible to me that there will be an end to it at all." He pressed his temples. "I feel really rotten."

"It serves you right," Jeanette said. "I'm not dumb."

Franz watched the door close, then looked all around before he covered his eyes again: at the Canadian railways travel posters on the walls, the old golden-oak bookcase in which, from the bed, he could see the Oz books and the Waverley Novels. What a typical and oppressing idea his father had had, to bring them all here and then to send him to this room. To have his son come with his wife to stay in the room where he had passed the years of his childhood. Yes, even to sleep with her in the bed where he had slept countless times alone. Who wanted the past linked to the present this way? Or any other?

Jeanette and Victoria arrived a short while after Monique had delivered Miriam's breakfast to her. Miriam had a parcel for the little girl with a dress and a sweater in it that would fit either now or later, she said, and another for Jeanette containing a very pretty Italian umbrella that she described as collapsing like a dead spider, which made it likely that Jeanette would never use it. And she gave Jeanette a check for two hundred dollars, out of what (with an apology for her facetiousness) she called "the sinking Baxter fund." In return, Miriam received two pretty silk scarves, for everybody knew of her fondness for scarves, stoles, shawls of every kind, and she was otherwise a hard person to buy a present for. Then the baby was put on the floor to crawl and bang a toy she'd got in her Christmas stocking and wouldn't let out of her hand, while Miriam ate her toast and drank her coffee and watched. When the tactful Monique tapped at the door and came in to get the tray, Victoria, stimulated, said a new word, a spittly mixture of vowels and a guttural. Jeanette pronounced it to be "Hugo" beyond any reasonable doubt.

"Then take her with you to see her grandfather, Monique, and see if she'll say it in front of him," Miriam said. "Nothing would please him more."

Monique put down the tray and gathered up the baby.

"I can take her to him," Jeanette said, quite willing to go, on first impulse.

"Either way," said Miriam.

But Jeanette, on second thought, found herself drawn to a dialogue with this—in the daytime it showed—this rather haggard woman. "If Monique doesn't mind . . ." she said.

"You must think you and I might have more things to say to each other," Miriam said, a remark Jeanette could interpret as friendly, and even, in a friendly way, willing. In any case, it did put the reason for staying out in front.

Miriam's upstairs retreat consisted of a sitting room, formerly the master bedroom of the house, a bath, and behind that, her bedroom, and then off that, over a part of the sun porch, still another room, more for spring and fall, once a sleeping porch but now glassed in; except for the absence of a kitchen, the retreat constituted an apartment. It was the first time Jeanette had ever been in it, although the house had already been arranged this way for a year or two when she and Franz came to visit at the time of their engagement. She was impressed by the retreat; her own parents shared a double bed and would till one of them died, and she found separate arrangements like these odd, cold, embarrassing, yet somehow elegant. Left alone with Miriam, and needing something to say, she remarked, looking around, "Why, it's such a pretty room, Mrs. Kerenyi. And you have a fireplace, too. That must be nice."

"I never use it. I've known too many people for whom fireplaces have connotations that annoy me." Miriam laughed. "As for the room, it's big rather than pretty, Jeanette. All deliberate."

"I love wicker," Jeanette said uncertainly.

"All right, all right. I like it myself. It doesn't collect germs, as my mother used to say when she hauled hers out to the driveway and hosed it off each spring and fall. It makes it seem as if I were in a house simplified for the summer, something very seasonal. But it's not the point, is it? I mean, we shouldn't be wasting time. Unless, of course, you prefer to."

"I don't think I know what you mean now."

"We've never talked, you and I, and I suppose we should. That's what I mean now. Once I promised you that we might one day. Have you forgotten?"

"Before my wedding. No, I haven't forgotten."

"I don't write letters any more and I don't like the telephone, so this may be your only chance for another four years, or ever, to ask me things. It's only fair that you get the chance. It is my obligation, not my pleasure. Do understand my motives."

Miriam stopped and Jeanette waited, too shy to say she didn't.

Miriam said, "I suppose I know aspects of your husband better than anybody else does. I have his causes at my finger tips, while you—you have the results on your hands. What would you like to know?"

Jeanette was dumb. As she might have guessed, this was going to be no cozy heart-to-heart talk between a mother-in-law and a daughter-in-law, but rather one of those awful contests which the whole Kerenyi family seemed to think of as normal conversation. Seconds passed. Miriam noticed that she was standing and motioned her into a chair placed at an easy distance, not too near, not too far from the wicker chaise longue, padded with pillows, on which she herself reclined.

"Ask something, Jeanette." Miriam smiled. "You'll make me nervous."

"Well . . ." Jeanette's voice was soft and fearful. "What was Franz like as a baby?"

"Good Lord, I don't remember—or much care. That won't do. Try again."

"I think you can tell a lot from that."

"Why then, I'll describe him for you, and you can see what you can tell. He ate. He slept. He cried. He wet.

Come, now . . . Let me try. How do you get along with my difficult son?"

"We love each other very, very much."

"Sweetly said."

"We're—happy."

"Can that really be true?"

"Naturally we have our troubles."

"Such was my impression. Judging from last night."

"I'm very proud of him. Everybody looks up to his mind. Not everybody likes him, but everybody respects him. He gets asked questions, if you know what I mean."

Miriam lighted a cigarette from a fan-shaped silver box beside her arm; pale cut stones set in the lid glittered when she opened it—surely a bit of Kerenyi bric-a-brac, never Baxter. Some smoke curled gracefully upward, ringing her head. "I'm not supposed to smoke because of last winter, but I allow myself two a day. Sometimes I think that is the greatest difference of all. Jeanette, we may as well stop right now if all you are going to do is to quote to me."

"Quote who? What?"

"I don't know. Magazines. Television plays. Books. I may be too condescending—or optimistic. I like the idea of your being impressed that people ask him questions, and for me it's a new way of thinking about him, too. But in general you are certainly not conveying anything much to me of what I guess life with Franzie must be like." She puffed, not, it appeared, inhaling, or almost not, never taking her eyes off Jeanette. "It is a question of how to put me to use. Not that I can solve any of your problems, or would want to. How you use me is up to you—if you use me at all. I don't want to volunteer things you don't need to hear or, as it may well be, don't want to."

And so Jeanette was presented with a choice: whether to take this strange, uncomfortable woman whose reputation for cleverness she'd encountered even at faraway

Stanford, into her confidence, treat her as a friend, even an ally, however provisionally, or whether to trust those instincts that told her that Miriam would never become such. It wasn't even that simple, for Jeanette could not feel Miriam as just one thing—a wit, given to irony and ridicule. She was drawn to Miriam, too, found in the mother some of the twists and turns and mysterious places that drew her to the son, and guessed that Miriam was various, and that one of her, at least, was sympathetic and warm—if she could but touch that one!

Moreover, Jeanette needed help and knew it. She chose to confide, and to that end, she gave an inch of discretion.

"Maybe this is what you want me to say to you, Mrs. Kerenyi: Franz is cross and hard to please."

"That's better."

"Impossible to please, sometimes. He acts as if nothing can be right."

"There are times when nothing is right, for Franz."

"Then again he's grateful for what I try to do—keep house, keep things quiet so he can work. You might say he's grateful to me for Victoria."

"Aren't you quoting once more? I never knew Franz to be grateful. Whatever comes to him is less than he's owed."

"It's just that he's so moody." When Miriam shook her head slowly, Jeanette felt very close to tears, perhaps because she was being pushed closer to truth. "What can I say, Mrs. Kerenyi? He's my husband."

"I'm only wondering now how much you've come to know."

"A lot. I was young when I married him. I've grown up."

Miriam asked slowly, "Just how bad is living with him, Jeanette?"

Jeanette felt the tears come closer, starting up in her eyes. As a Cotton born, she did not feel, as a Baxter might, that it was wrong to cry at all; but in front of this woman? "I don't know. I don't know how to answer that."

"Yes you do. Think. You have a perfect basis for comparison. You were raised in a family by a father and mother. I know you were because I met them. It's the yardstick, that experience, that all others have finally to be measured against."

"We're nothing like them, Franz and I, Mrs. Kerenyi. When they disagree, it isn't deep at all, any more than it is when I scold Victoria. And it's not much of the time. In that, they're like most other people. But not"—her voice sank to a whimper—"like Franz and me."

"Mostly not like Franz is what you mean."

"He's like a person with a backache—never, you know, comfortable. Yet I believe he loves me."

"He well may." Miriam puffed and puffed, concentrating seriously. "He very well may." Her feet shifted under the knitted throw that covered her legs as she turned a little farther onto her right elbow, but, as before, she didn't stop looking at Jeanette. "Do something," she said suddenly. "Blurt out to me, right now, right now without any qualifications, the worst single thing about being married to Franz. Blurt out what first comes into your mind. What is it?"

"I don't understand him."

"And what's the second? Come on. Quickly. Quickly."

"I'm afraid of him."

Jeanette stared at Miriam, frightened, now, by her own admissions.

Miriam said slowly, "That gives us enough to go on with, I'd think. What don't you understand about him?"

"Partly it's what he says. I don't even understand a lot of the words he uses, much less the sentences he uses them in; and he uses foreign words I don't understand—"

"You've seen where he picks all that up from."

"From his father, you mean. Yes, but he's like you in all that, too, Mrs. Kerenyi. And even when I understand the words I often don't understand his meaning. I don't know about the things he knows all about—history and philosophy and statistics. I only went through three years of college."

"Jeanette, I didn't even do that."

"I don't believe it."

"It's true. My father wanted his two daughters to be educated so that they would be the equals of any women in the country, and Dorcas did it—up to a point, when he, or she, realized—at least so I've always supposed—that her talents lay more . . . let us say in memory than in originality. But I got restless, moved around, didn't come near graduating. I chose a more active life. A typical radical of the thirties." Miriam seemed to be set adrift for the moment. "Bent on experiences, don't you know. I gave myself to all sorts of experiences, but never to love, until I met Hugo. Then I did that, too, and utterly without reservations, Jeanette. It's important for me to remember that. But I'm being selfish: back to you. No, I was hardly highly educated, in any formal sense. There. Does that make you feel better? Oh, I'll admit there are differences that matter between you and me, but I assure you that I, too, had to learn my way around in my husband's world, and in those days it was a world with its share of fabulous creatures, not just schoolteachers who had got above themselves. I was brought into that world; I didn't come from it." Miriam put out her cigarette with a kind of strong intent, really extinguished it, with a stab. "I will boast to you: I was never intimidated. There is perhaps the bigger difference between us. Frequently bored, often astonished, once in a while intoxicated, occasionally repelled, but never intimidated. There is surely the bigger difference."

"Because I am, you mean. Yes, I admit it. I am. By Franz and by the people we see, too. All of them like him, all the men, at least, and a lot of the women. All there is for me to do is to be quiet, or to talk to the wives about casseroles and schools and now Victoria. Mrs. Kerenyi, she's saved my life. I really do understand her."

"That will change too, I hope. But enough of your—let's call it educational diffidence. Tell me why you are afraid of him."

"Because of his mean streak."

"He doesn't—strike you?"

"No." Jeanette looked down at her hands, lying in her lap.

"But you think he might?"

"He drinks so much. When he does, you can't tell what he'll do, and he's very mean then."

"It's not easy to be your Franz; you know that."

"Of course I know that, though I don't know why. And I believe that without me it would be harder. I even know that the time may come when I'm the only person who will keep him going."

"Not an easy job now, and an unimaginable one then. I'm sure that's one of the things you know, too. Poor Jeanette. Perhaps now I should tell you some of the things I know."

"Could you tell me what I need to know to make it as easy as it can be? I don't expect it to be easy; I didn't when I married him; but sometimes I think it might be easier. For me. For Franz, too. Easier than it is."

"Don't sound pathetic. I don't like that."

Jeanette just looked at her.

Miriam said, "I can tell you, for instance, that Franz is a profoundly jealous man. Remember that. A jealous man. I'd as leave say envious. Between jealous and envious. He was jealous of Ann, and then later of the child that—died. Maybe other people. He's always, ever since I can remember, had this idea that he never gets his due. A boy gets into the habit of being jealous and envious, and then it's hard to break. And it gets directed more and more widely and takes on unexpected disguises, like a restless ambition that pricks a person to want to equal everyone in everything. It is not the same thing as being competitive, to strive against adversaries, try to win, because what is at stake in what I'm talking about is a little—unclean."

"He's very nasty about his colleagues, Mrs. Kerenyi. Sometimes."

"Mmm; I've never been quite sure Franz really wanted to be an academic at all. There's so much of his counterpoint with his father in it. He's chosen it, he's had to choose something, yet halfheartedly, and I think in some ways he'd rather be like—let's say like Bruce Cuttler. Or both. Both a historian and also the kind of man who marks up *The Wall Street Journal*, talks about dollars, millions of them, and snaps his fingers at headwaiters. Yet Franz doesn't really care about dollars in his heart, either, and he's too intelligent and self-conscious for all the rest."

"But what can I do about that?"

Miriam did not answer the question. Instead she went on. "So there's that about Franz: his envious streak, that leads him into pleasureless rivalry. Add that to the unhappy core of him. And then his lack of constancy in his ambitions, that he veers, won't ever be sure just quite what it is he wants. Some ambitious men have fixed goals and others have movable ones, as they say of feasts—I can never remember: are you Catholic? No. I didn't think so. Anyway, fixed and movable goals—that is a different way of talking about how he veers. Movable goals don't stay put or stay the same; they draw near and they recede. Never too far away not to beckon, or near enough to be achieved. What a hard life such a man must lead, when he can never have what he wants or even be sure what it is. And what a pity it is that Franz didn't learn some of the things Hugo could teach him by his example. I mean that one of Hugo's real strengths is that when he's done something, he really likes it. He isn't full of false vanity; he's got the real thing. The Hugo that Franz hears in his imagination, I would guess, is always telling him he ought to be doing something else and doing it better. But the real Hugo never tells himself that—unless he's on the verge of doing it. That's self-confidence, Jeanette, and it's lacking in Franz, for all his occasional boasting."

"He only boasts until you agree with him," Jeanette said, "and then he turns on you and says you don't know what you're talking about." She began to cry.

"Poor Jeanette. Poor, poor Jeanette."

"You've told me all this, Mrs. Kerenyi, but what can I do about it?"

"Why, I suppose what you *will* do is to stick by him as long as you can. And, inevitably, from time to time, cry."

"I'm sorry to cry. This really is helping. I can't go to my own mother, because she doesn't know what it's all about. She can understand the problems of a telephone-company employee, but—" Jeanette searched for a way to describe the chasm. "But not those of a man who reads eight languages."

"How fortunate that your father is not an international operator!" Miriam made a quick gesture of the hand. "Forgive me, Jeanette. I shouldn't joke. They will slip out."

"I think it will mean a lot to me to know that I can talk to you, now that we've broken the ice."

"We're a little far away from each other for that."

"Franz wants to move back East. To Harvard or Yale, or even back to Cornell. He'll succeed."

"I shouldn't be surprised. He's talented. It's hard for me to tell, with all that statistical business, those immigrant/emigrant units he writes about, as if the Russian Jews and Sicilian peasants were plankton clusters adrift on the Gulf Stream. It makes dull history for someone like me, but that's one of the things his colleagues will most like about it. A special language, incomprehensible to the laity."

Jeanette continued to test their new intimacy. "So we'll be closer to you. Maybe even Princeton . . ."

"I am sure there must be regulations against that. Fathers and sons."

"Well, anyway, Cambridge or New Haven. And we can see each other, or at least I'll talk to you on the telephone." Jeanette smiled. "Not for long at a time, since you don't like to. Maybe meet once or twice a year in New York for lunch and go to something. You see, it's being all alone with the problem of Franz that's hard to bear, him so unhappy. I need someone to say new things about him to me. I need my mother-in-law, Mrs. Kerenyi."

Jeanette sniffled and Miriam gave her a handkerchief that was tucked under a pillow of the chaise longue, then lay back and looked at her, but said nothing more until Jeanette began not to like the silence. Then she said, "Jeanette, I must be clear with you. This talk we've had: it is not a first one; it is a last one. You've imagined a way for me to be for which I have no vocation, and no inclination either. I have no intention of doing all that—meeting you in New York, chatting at Schrafft's and during the intermissions of a matinee. You have no right to ask it of me, either."

Jeanette, more guardedly, said over the handkerchief, "Some other way, then, that would suit you better."

"I offered information, but I did not offer to become involved. I do not want to be. Franz is yours, not mine."

"He's still yours too, Mrs. Kerenyi. Since we're telling each other things, I'll tell you that."

"I take a reasonable interest, Jeanette, in my son and in you and your problems. But no more. I'll not have all those chains fitted on me again."

"What an unbelievable thing to say about the feelings of a mother for her son and what happens to him. Chains!"

"I agree. There probably is a better word."

Jeanette was shy, not too articulate, but she was not abject. She said, "I wonder just what it is you've been doing talking to me this morning, Mrs. Kerenyi."

"In an indirect way, a small way, trying to be helpful."

"Not curious? You're sure not curious?"

"I was not being curious."

"I think so. You wanted to know about us. And to say ugly and somehow cold-blooded things about Franz and make me unhappy. And then to back away when you'd finished. Let me just tell you this: your advice without you behind it isn't worth anything at all."

"I haven't advised you to do anything."

"I'm beginning to understand a lot more than you would want about what's gone wrong with my husband."

"Then, in the end, we haven't wasted our time."

"What's been wasted in this room is something a lot more precious than time."

"Love proffered, you mean? Quoting again, Jeanette. And suppose you did arouse some of the feelings in me you have been trying to arouse. What good would it do? I could only stand on the side lines, at best."

"Don't worry. Whatever happens to us will be without you or anybody else in his family."

"Jeanette, I will not be drawn back into the world of impossible relationships, quarrels and conciliations, not to mention sabbaticals and promotions and valentines and Mother's Day cards."

"I hope I never grow out of being human."

Miriam shrugged. "So it's not just you. At least you do understand that."

"Of course. I'm just—" Jeanette searched for a phrase of her own, and her eye fell upon the breakfast tray that Monique had had to leave behind. "I'm just what's on your plate for nine-thirty Christmas morning, that's all."

Miriam said, "Quite true. And henceforth you are all by yourself with that which you, after all, have brought to pass. It's a reminder we all need."

Jeanette, frowning and angry, stood up to go. Like any underdog, she knew when she had nothing to lose. She turned around from the door. "Poor Professor Kerenyi," she said.

"Which one?" Miriam replied.

She did not move until Jeanette had closed the door.

Then she held up one of her hands and watched it. It was shaking, as much as one of Grandfather Kerenyi's. She sat up higher and bent over the arm of her chaise longue so that she could see the breakfast tray and its empty plate.

"The poor little thing," she said aloud.

Ann caught Monique Lupiac in the third-floor hall, just as Monique was about to go into her room. Ann said, "Father tells me you won't be having dinner with us today, that you're going to New York." Monique nodded. "Could we possibly talk a little now? You can imagine why."

"Of course, Mrs. Cuttler." The girl gestured at her door and then at the one opposite. "In my room or in yours?"

Ann said, "Yours. We won't be interrupted." She smiled. "And it's the household from the point of view of your room I want to know about."

They went there, and Ann looked around. "Most of this furniture is familiar," she said. "Furniture tends to float upwards, doesn't it? I first remember that useless little table in the living room, then in the back hall downstairs, then the second floor, maybe in my own bedroom by that time, and finally here. But a newish desk."

"And a new bed, they told me. Lots of new things," Monique said. "Lamps, and the little refrigerator. Your father and mother have been very generous."

"They can be that." Ann sat down in an armchair, and Monique sat at the foot of the bed, sinking into the down comforter folded there. "I take it that you have been, well, more or less received into the family, Monique. And so you must know what has been happening around here better than I do. I know what I've been told, but you can tell me what it really was, perhaps."

"I don't know all that much," Monique said.

Ann appraised her: she lacked freshness; it happened with such dark coloring sometimes. Voluptuous but scarcely dewy, this girl. "Look, I don't want you to tell me

anything that would make your own position more difficult—and I don't mean just if I repeated it. I mean more
difficult in your own mind, too."

Monique nodded slowly.

"You weren't living here when I was here last winter,
when my mother was so sick. When did you come?"

"In June. I lived downstairs, in the room your aunt is in
now, while your father was in Europe. So that I could hear
if your mother called."

"And did she?"

Monique smiled. "Not in that way."

"Do you find my mother strange or difficult?"

"Yes, of course."

"Yes, of course. Ah . . . I see. I wonder, can you imagine what she was once like?"

"Yes. And I've heard, too. But you know, Mrs. Cuttler,
she's no less—fine, now. It's only that she's so—I don't
know how to put it—so turned away from so many things
and people. It's caused a lot of bad feelings. But I don't
think that's why she's done it."

"That's one of the things that bother me." Ann nodded.
"It would be a lot easier for me to deal with this situation if
only I could imagine her acting from malice or spite. But
you know, Mother never did do that."

"No, no," Monique said. "It isn't malice."

"No. Unfortunately, it's something we must respect."

"She's a very wonderful person."

"That, too. But perhaps for that reason, she's always, not
just now but always, been hard on her supporting cast."

"Why should you expect that to change?"

"I don't. What do you think about my father?"

"He's a wonderful person, too."

"He's certainly filled with self-pity these days."

"He has a great deal to be sorry for himself about, Mrs.
Cuttler."

"What? Surely not the fact that Mother didn't come

down to observe my children tearing apart an old pair of
Aunt Dorcas's lisle stockings in their haste to get their
hands on their caramels."

"Oh, no, though that may be harder on him than you
think. But more than that. His life has been hard for him
this fall. I don't like to put it this way, but it's the truth: he
has been humiliated. In front of students, once. She
walked out, came back, and then disappeared during a
party he gave here for his seminar. They noticed it. Students gossip. And they look for faults in their professors—
it's the other side of admiring them. He goes everywhere
alone, but everybody knows she *could* go if she wanted to.
They say that it's with him she won't do it. When I'm
asked, I can't even deny it. It's the truth."

"So then you take my father's side."

"No." Monique looked right into Ann's eyes, so point-
edly that Ann began to distrust her. "Mrs. Cuttler, I'm
caught in between. I've been caught right in between. He
has his grievances. She has a right to her own ways. I live
here. I like, almost love them, both equally." The eyes did
not drop, even on that.

"What do you project for the future?"

"It's a household without a center to it," Monique said,
bringing Ann up with the precision of her description. "I
don't think that will get better."

"And what can I do about it?"

Monique thought for quite a while. "Nothing. Leave
them alone."

Ann said, more forcefully, "But I'm their daughter. How
can I sit and see all this happen—whatever it is?"

"You don't have to. You will be in Chicago."

"But I can't shrug it all off, Monique. There must be
something I can do to bring them back to their senses."

"They haven't lost them."

"You defend the *status quo*, then?"

"I accept it."

"I don't give up like that. I'll manage something," Ann

said. "I don't intend to leave this house in the same condition I found it in, I promise you, if I can help it."

"As you said this morning to your father, it might get worse, Mrs. Cuttler."

"Have you anything else to say to me?"

The girl shook her head.

"Do you know what I think?" Ann got up, her manner rather brisk. "I think you're too wound up in this place, in what's been happening here, to see clearly. I can understand that, Lord knows. I was wound up in it myself for a good many years. We've traded niches, haven't we, in that sense. Beware, Monique. That's my advice to you, in exchange for yours to me. They are dangerous people, particularly for the young. Just ask my brother. Everett Pinckney—do you know him? You must know who he is— once described them as Circe and the Hussar. There's truth at the bottom of that. Two dangerous kinds of allure, you see."

Monique got up too. "I'm sorry I can't help."

"Well, I'm grateful to you for talking to me, anyway." Ann paused and shot a quick look at the girl, and again their eyes met. "What a responsibility for a girl of twenty-four. To be caught just exactly, mathematically, between Mother and Father, in this crazy old house. A very important part to play, Monique. But be careful. The slightest deviation from true north and you are compromised. Now I'll go and let you get dressed."

Ann left, with the feeling that she did not quite like Monique, and it certainly seemed to her that Monique must feel the same way. Well, she wasn't of much use, anyway. Only a minor complication, really, whatever she was up to. Unessential, but a complication.

Miriam put down her book and removed her glasses in order to watch Monique approach her chaise longue.

"How you do glide, Monique. I've seen older women who've developed a glide like that, usually, I think, because they fear that otherwise they'd hobble. Never a girl your age before."

"I've come to say good-by, Mrs. Kerenyi. And to wish you a Merry Christmas again and give you this." Monique held out a small package.

Miriam felt it. "Cigarettes! Am I right? Those wonderful dark Turkish ones you brought me the other time?" She began to take off the paper. "Just smell them. Incense. This should be Twelfth-day, not Christmas."

"I know they're bad for you, but as long as you will smoke anyway, I think you might as well smoke what you really like."

"Quite right. Six boxes of them. At two a day that will last me months. I'll space them out—odd days only. How wonderful. And here is something for you. Forgive its impersonality, but it will be useful." Miriam handed the girl an envelope. "I'm glad you don't have to have all your Christmas meals here and can speak French at at least one of them."

Monique smiled. "It's quite possible my aunt will be the only other person there who speaks French."

"That's all you will need." Miriam had an idea. She took the package Jeanette had brought in to her and lifted out one of the silk scarves. "Take this with you. Put it on when you're away from the house. It was chosen to look well on me, and we're rather alike—as I used to be. It'll look very nice with your dark-blue dress. Only don't wear it back. Shove it in a pocket until they've gone home—young Franz and his wife. But put it on now, if you like. Use the mirror back there. Your coat will cover it as you leave."

Miriam sat up and turned around in order to watch the girl knot the scarf. "How deft you are. The house will seem quiet tomorrow, won't it? Especially your part of it."

"I won't mind."

"I should think not."

"It will seem more like my own again." Monique smiled by way of the mirror. "They're good children."

"My daughter Ann is stern. More so than her father, more so than I. She's a successful alloy."

Monique nodded and turned around, finished. "How does it look? Well?"

"Lovely. Here. Take the other one, too. Why waste it on me when it can adorn youth?"

Monique's heavy, straight brows contracted a little. "It's different," she said. "What are you going to do today, Mrs. Kerenyi? Will you go down to dinner?"

"It's funny. You're the first person who's asked me."

"They've thought of it already. Mrs. Cuttler did. She's quick, and—yes, stern. Very strong-minded. It would be hard to hold out against her indefinitely. Can you?"

"Let's just think about dinner. You know, I haven't decided. I keep feeling I must teach my family by more examples. But there is old Mr. Kerenyi."

Monique said, "Yes, he is so charming. It will be a good dinner, I think. Mrs. Vendredy has been busy at it for the last hour. A good dinner may be worth a compromise."

"Your French quarter speaking."

Monique smiled. "Well, I've got to hurry for my bus now. Thank you for this—and for the scarves."

She pulled the collar of her coat up high as she left the room, to conceal the scarf from anybody she chanced to meet in the hallway. It wasn't a bad idea anyway, for it was exceedingly cold, well below freezing, even toward the middle of the day, with a wind out of the northwest. It would be a cold walk to the bus stop and a cold wait. Had she turned around, she would have seen Miriam Kerenyi in her front window, watching her, off the chaise longue at last. Miriam had come to verify that when Monique got a hundred feet or so from the house, her walk would change. It did. She no longer glided, but walked with spring to her step, a usual kind of walk. And then there was a sound downstairs and Hugo rushed out of the house. He called to Monique. He would drive her to her bus. He got the keys to his car and she came to it and got in and they drove off.

When the car disappeared around a corner, Miriam returned to her chaise longue. She went once around it, trying
to glide like Monique, a second time at a livelier gait,
smiled, and lay down once more to await her next visi-
tor.

Ann, too, noticed Hugo going after Monique. She
wanted to ask him more about the girl, now that she was
out of the house, but there wasn't time to wait for him to
come back. She had to go up to her room and get on her
warmest clothes, for she and Bruce were going to take the
children for a drive and a walk on this bitter morning, over
through the campus to see the university buildings there.
Bruce was already in their room, pulling on a sweater, and
so Ann at least could talk to him and tell him something of
her conversations with her mother, and of her impressions
of Monique:

"Unessential, but a complication."

"A sexy complication," Bruce said.

"Nice enough looking. Not—healthy, somehow."

"Sexy," he repeated. "I don't suppose that's got anything to do with your mother—no doubt Dorcas got all
those hormones—but I wouldn't be so sure about your father."

"Bruce, you really are impossible. I won't have you talking that way."

"Sometimes I think I'll break you of the family habit of
refusing to notice the obvious, and sometimes I think I'll
never succeed." He put on his jacket and got his scarf and
some fleece-lined gloves he'd packed. "Do you know what
I'd like to do right now? I'd like to go over and look at that
girl's room. Do you suppose she locked it?"

"Did you use to?"

"No, never. I don't think there was a key to the door, and
there certainly hasn't been one made since. Come on.
Come with me while I have a quick look at it on our way
out."

"We shouldn't," Ann said, "should we?"

"Why not? I don't mean to go through her drawers. That isn't the reason I want to see it."

They tried the door. It wasn't locked. They went in.

Bruce looked around. "New desk," he said. "And new bed."

"You're right. She mentioned both. We did."

"I'll bet they got rid of both the old ones after we left here. To show how much they disapproved of my mind, in the case of the desk, and of us, in that of the bed."

Ann stared at him. "You amaze me. I'll bet you're right. Something like that. That girl knew they were new, so maybe your timing is off—eight years or so. Or maybe they didn't bother to replace them right away, since they never replaced you either, until her."

He laughed. "Let's try this bed out. Let's be the roomer and the professor's daughter again."

"Bruce!"

"Oh, I don't mean *that*. Come on." He was grinning.

She said of him, "Lewd and diabolical."

"Come on. Just try it. See if they replaced the one we learned on with a screwproof model. Come on."

"But it's hers. And we'll rumple it."

"And straighten it up again. Come on." He took Ann's hand and pulled her along with him, kicked off his shoes, which hadn't laces, lay down, and pulled her onto the bed beside him. She was stiff and resisting, but he made her turn to him and they embraced. After a while he said, "We never have had better times than right here."

"No. Is it because I was so desperate?"

"So was I. No. It's because it was new. We were new to each other. And then, it was so nice and sneaky, and they had it coming."

"In a way, yes."

He kissed her again. "It's been as good, but never better," he said.

"You rescued me."

"You know, Annie, I'm conceited, but one thing I've never thought was that if I hadn't, you wouldn't have found another way out of this house."

"But not up to this room."

"Should we . . . ?"

"Absolutely not."

"Prude. Your father wants to make the past and present come together. Well, let's."

"Idiot. What a trick to play on him. And on that girl."

"And don't forget your mother."

"You can almost make me forget that I love them—except for the girl, of course. Come on, we've got to go downstairs or the children will come up for us and catch us here."

They got off the bed and carefully straightened it.

"I wonder," Ann said, "if Father ever described you as a sexy complication."

On the way downstairs, Bruce stopped outside Miriam's room. He sent Ann on to get the children ready, said he'd follow in a few minutes, knocked and opened Miriam's door.

"I'm next, Miriam," he said. "Have you had a chance to change the sheet on the examination table?"

Miriam said, "For you or for me?"

"We'll see. I won't be long; we're just about to go out. Ann's told me of her conversations with you, and it brought some questions to my mind."

"Sit down, Bruce. No matter how brief you make your questions, you can't be sure that my answers will be such that you'll want to stand through them."

He did so, and stretched out his long legs, with the self-satisfaction of a young man who is both handsome and rich; inevitably diminishing in the first, he was as surely augmenting in the second. "I'll begin with a statement. You know that Hugo raised heaven and hell to get us all here this Christmas."

"And in which did he find you?"

Bruce smiled. "I'm not so sure you've changed at all, old girl."

"Bruce, I do not like insolence masked as familiarity."

"Anyway, he did, and I agreed to it. I agreed because I had the feeling that whatever was going on here might, if it wasn't tuned down, if he wasn't, that is, end by affecting my life through affecting Ann's."

"Self-interest rather than a mercy errand."

"What has Hugo ever done to deserve mercy?"

"Never to have asked for it."

"We could go on like this, but I don't intend to; there's serious business to get done. I'll be frank and tell you what I think I'm up against. You have the problems of those who can afford them, Miriam. Affluent women can afford to suffer from ennui; poor ones can't. If you knew my family you'd know what I mean, and perhaps know why I'm not very patient in this house. There, with my family, you can see the real problems that come from improvidence of every kind—economic being only one of them. Not that that makes them any less boring."

"There is a saying that the only true philosopher is one with a full belly, Bruce. That should point out to you some of the ways your upbringing may have limited your values."

"I've come here, in any case, to put some ordinary words to your situation, and ask you some obvious questions. Isn't the heart of it just that you and Hugo are not getting along?"

"Quite wrong. I am not disagreeing with him, though he may be with me."

"If you will say yes, I'm not going to tell you you're wrong. I'm surprised you didn't drop him a long time ago. You're brighter in every way than he is, I think. I remember in one of the bigger arguments he and I had before Ann and I left here, he said that the life of the spirit and the intellect—his words, not mine—were the main

ring of the circus, and the money-getters and -lenders
were only in one of the side shows. It's always seemed to
me that if this family has a main ring, you're in it, Miriam,
not Hugo. So why shouldn't you drop him? My objection
would be to the way that you've chosen to do it. Slowly
and painfully. No doubt it's full of satisfactions for you, but
it's going to take a long time and upset everybody com-
mensurately. Change that and you can do as you please.
I'm not trying to persuade you that Hugo is lovable."

"And am I?"

"Certainly more than Hugo."

"Shouldn't you be saying most of this to him, then? In
any case, you are wrong."

"Mmm. Maybe. How about your health? Is that really
all right?"

"So far as I know it is fine. I've not recovered all my
strength since—"

"So I've heard. What does your doctor—what's his
name? Skinner?—what does he say?"

"That there's nothing wrong with me."

"You're sure. You're sure he's being honest with you.
And with Hugo. Both of them with you. You're sure you
aren't growing a cancer or carrying around a leaky heart—
one of those things that take away people's energy to keep
going on? Your innards are all right?"

"Talk to Doctor Skinner."

"I just might."

"You'd better ask Hugo first. I don't care what you do,
but I know him. He wouldn't like it."

"What do I care? Let me ask you another question. You
don't have a new playmate, do you?"

"Playmate?"

"Lover, if you prefer."

Miriam laughed. "At my age and with my disposition?
Bruce, you really do have a market-place imagination."

"It happens everywhere, all the time."

"Not, I hope, in your house."

"Don't worry about Ann. I'll always take care of her, because she's mine."

"I'd put it differently, my lad."

"What about alcohol?"

"It doesn't work with me. It's a problem born into people, I think."

"Well, it was born into Franz, and he must have got it from somebody."

"That will do. Anyway, in my new state I am rather joyous than melancholy—I believe. So why be an alcoholic?"

"When you were sick last winter did they ever put you on drugs? Morphine?"

"You're very up-to-date."

"I know someone's wife. She daydreams, too. At other times, I have to admit, she's not much like you."

"It isn't a chemical enemy you've got for yourself."

"Obviously you couldn't tell me if you were crazy. It's a possibility."

"I doubt that you'd get far in a court."

"What's wrong, Miriam? You tell me."

Miriam thought for a long time. At length she replied, "Each person who asks me that, Bruce, deserves a different reply. I have yours. What is wrong with me? The answer to you, with your view of life, is: nothing."

"That word keeps turning up, and it's not—" He stopped when a child's voice called him from the hall: Daddy, daddy. He stood up. "Ann's got the children ready. We're going over to show them where, but for a few strokes of luck, a touch of skepticism, above all some common sense and prudence, their papa might be working for fourteen thousand a year right now. 'Nothing' is a word, and an idea, I don't believe in. There's something, all right, behind all this. Maybe I can't find out. I'll try. I'll check your answers, if it's possible."

"Do. If it is."

"You haven't gone and got religion, have you, Miriam?"

"I don't need it."

"A couple of things you said last night about that child of yours who died of exposure made me wonder."

"Never fear. It's just . . . nothing."

"Maybe my Christmas present to myself," Bruce said in leaving, "will be to provide 'nothing' with its true name."

"Oh, it's you, Dorcas. Come on in," Miriam said. "Do we have anything left to say to each other after last night?"

Dorcas held out a small package. "I wanted to give you this. A book."

"And I have something for you. Also a book." Miriam got up and got it off a table. "I didn't wrap it."

"But it's the family album."

"I know. I thought you ought to have it for a while. Someday you can pass it on to Ann. Or Franz. If you want."

Dorcas took the old brown volume, tooled to look like leather, stamped *Family Album* on its front cover in gold. It was filled with ancient photographs, a few clippings and cards, some letters. "Look at that. Just look," she said, turning a couple of pages. Then she closed it abruptly. "All those Baxter faces, and the Tewkes faces and Ogden faces and the Pierce faces. They wouldn't much approve of what you've been doing, Miriam."

"They wouldn't understand it. I'll concede that."

"Staying in your room this morning. Not a one of them would ever have done that who could get onto her feet at all. Your grandchildren filling the house, too. Not to mention the rest of what you've been doing. It's quitting, I think. That's not the way the Baxters do things."

"So you're going to take Hugo's side."

"You can't say I do it often."

"Don't do it now."

"Oil and water. Oil and water," Dorcas said.

"What do you mean?"

"They won't mix, of course. There was your mistake.

You insisted on trying it. Well, now you've got to be ready to pay the price."

Miriam said, "Let's not talk any more. Let's leave the friendliness of last night still in the air between us, Dorcas."

"I can't feel right about it if I don't speak my mind. I want you to know what I think. Baxters see things through."

"And that is what I'm doing."

"It is not! You're sound in mind and sound in body, and you've got duties and should do them. Well, I'll go. I've said it. I've tried. You're coming to dinner, I hope."

"I don't know."

"If you don't, Hazel will probably be insulted, being so sensitive already about feeling herself an outsider here. I won't have that. I wish she wasn't coming over, but she is, and I won't have you insult her. I've got to go now and meet her, out at the Junction." Dorcas hugged the Baxter album close. "I don't like the way things are here, I'll tell you that. Not that it's all your fault, not all of it. A lot of it is Hugo. With Hazel to back me up, I may just give him a piece of my mind, too. But things have come to a pretty pass when the lady of the house doesn't show up on Christmas morning, that's all I can say."

Miriam said, "Dorcas, don't judge where obviously you don't understand."

"Oh, fiddlesticks." Dorcas stopped, a hand on the door-knob. "Do you know what Hugo gave me for Christmas?"

"No. What?"

"A vaporizer. To fill the air with steam."

"I suppose he thought one might be useful in your little apartment."

"There's a meaning behind it, some kind of dig at me. Poking fun. I'm sure of that. Hazel might guess. She'll know what they say about them in their advertising; they sell them in better drugstores—and there's that, too. Anyway, it'll be something derogatory, I'm sure of it. A vaporizer! I get tired of books, as if that's all I ever could want for Christmas or all I could ever use, but any book, including the Bible, would have been better than a vaporizer, I can tell you. I'm not yet all that dried out."

"Calm down, Dorcas. That's not what he meant, I'm sure. I had to have one here when I got out of the hospital, and he got one for his own study. You're overwrought. Christmas does funny things to everyone."

Dorcas weighted each syllable of her last sentence. "I sincerely hope I shall have the pleasure of seeing you at dinner, Sister."

Toward noon young Franz Kerenyi felt better. That meant that he had to go in and see his mother, but first he sought out his wife, who had not spoken to him after she'd seen Miriam, and he had not wanted to ask her about it then, either. She was back in the kitchen fixing something for Victoria—one of the seemingly endless bottles or purées—and he took her out to the pantry, where Mrs. Vendredy and her niece couldn't hear.

"How did it go? With Mother? I'm on my way myself."

Jeanette said, "She is a terrible, terrible person. I will never come back here again after we leave. That's how it went."

Franz sucked his breath in through his teeth. "That bad?"

"I cried in front of her," Jeanette said, mentioning the thing that, in retrospect, humiliated her the most.

"Why?"

"Ask her. I won't tell you."

"Well, I hope you didn't let her best you too easily."

Jeanette just looked at him for a moment, then turned and went back to the kitchen.

Franz climbed the back stairs up to the second floor, stopped to get a magazine out of his suitcase, and went forward to the door of Miriam's sitting room. He knocked and went in, trying to appear as casual as possible. He tossed the magazine onto her table, right by Miriam's hand.

"It's my latest article—in the *Cahiers d'études démographiques.*"

"You've waited till very late to come and see me," she said, putting it to one side.

"I expect you're all talked out by now. What did you say to Jeanette to make her cry?"

"I fancy she cries a lot."

"Yes, she does. Still, there's often some kind of reason."

"You'll have to ask her."

"I did. She said to ask you."

"Then you'll never know."

Franz moved restlessly around the room, picking things up, putting them down. It was a trick out of childhood, this handling things, that he had mostly educated himself away from, but in here the impulse was irresistible. He said, as he moved, "Did you really read my book?" He picked up the book from Dorcas, still wrapped.

"I did."

"What did you think of it?" He put the book down, moved along, picked up a small lacquer bowl that had some burns in the bottom from cigarettes.

Miriam did not watch him. Knowing what he was doing, she stared straight ahead. "Well, you know . . ."

"It had a little elegance, I think." Down went the bowl.

"Yes. And somewhere in it was something about me."

"About you?" He turned toward her, surprised.

"In one of all those tables must have been concealed my great-great-grandfathers."

"I'm very probably going to get a prize. The Francis Parkman."

"Will the honor make you happy, Franz?"

He snorted his quick, uninfectious laugh. "Very." He moved along, stopped, lifted the corner of a small rug with his toe. "Just what is it you're up to, Mother?"

"We get down to that. I'm almost tired of the question."

"Father's letters have been rather despairing."

"I'm just doing what I want to do for a change."

"No wonder there's been such an uproar."

"Think what an opportunity it will be for him to develop."

"I'd be careful of using irony when dealing with Father."

"Perhaps I meant exactly what I said."

"Develop? He's more likely to explode." Franz came to stand right behind her. "Mother, are you really all right? Your health and all? Really?"

"Yes, I am."

"Father said you probably hadn't read my book."

"Did he? Surely just some old fear of his speaking. I'll even read this article, if I can find the words I don't know in my French dictionary."

"Do you think about Nicky much? What you said last night about jealousy wasn't fair. After all, I was the one who was with him. I know what morbid recollections are."

"I know that. No, not much."

"What I remember is the funeral. I cried, I remember, and was ashamed, because I thought I was too old to. And I watched you all the time. I can remember that the clearest of anything. I can see myself watching you. Do you know what I mean? Do you have memories of yourself when you were a child, looking at yourself doing something from outside? I think it must be unusual. I should look it up. Anyway, that's what I remember. Me, the way I looked, a runt then, too, and redheaded, naturally, and I had on a new dark suit you'd bought me for dances. And from somewhere or other you'd found a boy's black four-in-hand. Imagine a mourning necktie for a boy of fourteen. I suppose it was left from some school uniform. And I had that on, and I kept pulling at it, at the narrow end, tucked underneath, and looking down at it when I wasn't watching you." His fingers made noise, picking at the fibers of the high back of the chaise longue. "So I wouldn't get caught staring at you, because I suppose I thought that in some way it was the wrong thing to do. I was reading every tiny sign in your face, Mother. And do you know what impressed me most of all? You looked the same to me. You even smiled at us, Annie and me, when we were supposed to do something and Aunt Dorcas gave us the order. Get up and go out, or go away from the graveside, I don't know what it was. I couldn't understand then, and I suppose I still can't, why you didn't seem to care more about Nicky's dying, as you had so favored him when he was alive."

"It was for your sakes. Especially you, because it wasn't your fault."

"Wasn't it?"

"One isn't surprised that a fourteen-year-old is careless. I knew the danger of your thinking so, and I tried to be careful. I don't think I favored him all that much, Franz. That was your interpretation. He was so much younger. He took attention."

Franz began to move around again. "It was more than that. With him there, after he was born, I felt more and more hopelessly that there wasn't anybody I could turn to."

"And now you have somebody. Jeanette is so evidently a person you can turn to."

"And you're backing out."

"You couldn't turn to me now anyway."

"I never could. I resent what's happening to you just because it's so reminding."

"Franz, what is the good of tallying up an old account once again?"

"Because it's as if it was all happening again, what happened to me during what I call my Jesuit years, you know, the ones they say that if they can have you for them they have you from then on." Franz stopped in front of the mirror. "Because you know, you have done this before. This backing out."

"What do you mean?"

"All the swagger and energy and all the other things that you married Father for—they wore thin before, too. And what you did when you backed out before was to hand me over to Father. That was your way of doing it. You let him have his way, let me be his, the first-born, all that crap, gave me over to him. All I can remember is doing things with him; I don't remember doing things with you, only wanting to. When Nicky came along, it was just that much worse. Maybe the two were close together, maybe even related. You and Ann and Nicky might do one thing, go one place, but I'd go another. Like ice skating. We're going to have to do that today. It's too much. He's got skates for the Cuttler kids; he's got all the things arranged already. You'd take Nicky and Ann and go to one place but I'd have to go with Father and try to skate faster and faster and faster and faster and on and on and on and on and on. How's that for something symbolic? Only it isn't. It's the literal truth. I was scared. It was too fast and too far for me, really was, but he didn't notice and didn't care. It was up to me to match his pace. You threw me to him so that you could get away from him yourself, so that you could do as you pleased. Not *care* for him, do you see? So that you could back out. I'm the result of some primal act of sacrifice on your part, Mother."

He could barely hear her reply. "You have my trait of exaggerating."

"And now you're backing out again, this time, I suppose, permanently. And the rest of us are going to have to pick up the pieces. He'll have to, too—to pick up the ones he can find. The ones he even recognizes. You're caving in once more, just the way you did. Who's going to be your sacrifice this time?"

"There's nobody left."

"Or else it's all of us. Annie, me, our families, and Father, too. We're all to be victims."

"What terrible things you are saying to me."

"I intend them to be. I intend to say the things nobody has ever said. You think that you think of everything, and, more or less, you do. More or less. But people who think of everything where what they do is concerned, and what other people do, who understand everything and see over and beyond and under and around everything the way you do—there's always something those people don't see. And it's right at the heart of all they do see. They don't see what is wrong that is at the exact center out of which they see up, down, around, and over. That's why they don't see it, because it's coexistent with them. Do you know what it is that's there in your case, Mother? I'll tell you. A simple human deficiency. Not vanity, as a lot of your friends might say, but a lack of love. It's a failure to love other people quite enough. If you'd loved me enough you'd have fought for me against Father. If you'd loved him enough, he might not, *might* not, have wanted me."

"Where did you learn all this?"

"From a bottle—because that's what I am, or what I'm getting to be; I'm not going to be one of the ones who don't admit it. With some people, there's a time when their poison acts for illumination. When I get drunk by myself, when I can't bear whatever state of being it is I have to bear that is unbearable, when that happens, there's a point in between the unbearable and the oblivion when I see things rather clearly. Now I've told you some of the things I've seen. The landscape of the past that I look out on then is not a very pretty one; it's littered with bones. I see either grinning faces or dead ones. There aren't any flowers, Mother, and the light is cold. Why do you think I write about whole populations, masses of people going from here to there, staying or going on? Villages and crowded piers and shipfuls, so many babushkas to the cubic yard of hold space, Conestoga wagons and third-class carriages, immigrant sheds and tenement houses? It's because as individuals, they might grin at me. They can't grin at me as long as they're stuffed into steerage."

"My God, Franz."

"One person is going to know what you are up to, and is going to judge you for it rightly. I know what you're up to."

"I think you had better go. And had better know that even this . . . this grotesque version of our family past, and the interpretations it has led you to, will not, would not if I accepted it, make me change my mind."

"But it has shocked you?"

"Not into caring. There."

Franz said, "It may be a long time before we talk to each other again. It's too bad our conversation has had to be like this, Mother. I don't take the blame for that."

"Yes, it is too bad. You turn out to be more . . . interesting than I had ever imagined."

"I'm more interesting right now than when I came into this room. Not that I was making it up as I went along, though I'd never quite put it all together as I just did. But what I'd never have foreseen was that you wouldn't at least try to deny it—to fight it down."

"I refuse, for you or anyone else, to get drawn, by anybody's judgments, back into the terrible human business of trying to be better."

"Fair enough."

He waited. Miriam did not speak. He changed to a different, a breezier manner. "I'm off to get myself the first drink of the day. I need it. I've been needing it. See you later, Mother. See you later," he said.

Old Mr. Kerenyi said, "I came up to get you. I thought we might talk a bit and then go down to dinner together—the company is assembling. And I had this for you."

Miriam opened the package he held out to her. It contained a book which, unlike the Baxter album, was bound in full fine leather and carefully tooled in gold—several fine lines of varying widths paralleling the edges, and then, in the center field, a series of tiny sunbursts—and the edges of the pages gilded, too. She ran her hand over it. "The binding is so sumptuous I feel no curiosity to see what is inside," she said.

"Yes. I had it done in New York. Years ago I occasionally used to get books bound there—my beautiful *Buddenbrooks*, you remember it? They are still in business up near Columbus Circle. Almost the only place."

Miriam opened it. "A blank diary!" she exclaimed. "I've never kept one."

"You must start." He smiled, watching her reactions. "It is for five years. It will run through nineteen seventy-three."

"You are an old fox," she said. She turned the pages. "Sunday, May the third, nineteen-seventy. Wednesday, July the twenty-fifth, nineteen-seventy-three. What a clever way to pass a sentence of longevity."

"Precisely. I thought this was a way of making you aware of my daily command to continue, even though I do not doubt that one of the pages well before the end will carry a droll entry in it about the last joke to be played on me."

"I'll let you write it yourself, the day before."

"Annie, my beloved Annie, has been talking to me a little just now," he said. "Her cheeks were bright from their walk into the campus. She was very . . . full of life. I saw no reason, from what she told me, not to give you the diary. I hope I was right."

"I'll keep it as long as I can, Franz," Miriam said.

"There are blank pages, too, at the end. You can go on into nineteen-seventy-four."

"Just as long as I can."

Mr. Kerenyi bowed. "That is all I can ask."

"You know, I haven't yet decided whether or not I'll go down to dinner, Franz. I've talked to everybody I needed to talk to. If I do, it will be because of you. Yet, why? I've been wondering to myself why I should feel quite that way about you. I think it's because you are so fastidious with people. You handle them like a clerk in a silver shop. You always put on your white gloves first."

"It is a kind of coldness."

"I like that, too. People full of human warmth tend so often to want reflectors for it so they can get its benefit."

"But will you come down? Am I that powerful?" the old man asked, smiling. He made a little face. "Not to, on Christmas, in your own house—that would be exaggerated."

"And to go may be deceitful. You see, Franz, it would be very easy to pass these few hours—yesterday, today, tomorrow—going through forms. Honoring the terms of what Hugo has called our pact—as if just that word weren't enough to make me want to break them. 'Pact'! But how can I let Ann and Franz come and go without learning anything? Really learning. I have to convince them. If I can't, I won't be able to convince myself."

"Of what, Miriam? Of what?"

"That everything I've been saying this morning is true and as I want it to be. I must convince them of that in order to make myself believe in it. That is almost the hardest thing of all."

He clung, as old people do, to a small point. "Yes, but Christmas dinner?"

She gazed at him. "Old friend," she said, "it is no more likely to be your own last than my own. Well . . . I will do it. I will go with you."

"Just one question. One question. I have no right to ask it, but may I?"

She was on her way back into her bedroom. She paused. "Of course."

"Well, you know," he said, "some of the important things we do require us to be brave. At other times, we are wise to be cowards. The idea is a commonplace. Nevertheless, I would like to ask you just this: is whatever it is that is happening to you requiring of you that you be brave, or that you be cowardly?"

"What a wonderful question, Franz! And so like you. Let me think." She did so. Then she said, "I can give an answer. My answer is: neither. If I do it well and wisely and as I want to: neither. It is just all"—she touched the edges of her hands together at the height of her waist, then slowly moved them apart, palms down—"level. Like that. Flat."

"That can't be. Everything that we do has texture. It is at the center of life itself."

"Flat, quite flat," she said.

"So. Well, go ahead, then. We'll be late as it is. Get dressed. I will wait for you."

She disappeared, and he went to the front windows and sat where he could look out, right through the branches of the oak trees into the amazing blue sky of a bright winter day. But Miriam, after a while, came back to tell him that she had changed her mind, that she couldn't, no she simply couldn't, and wouldn't, go downstairs with him. He argued gently, but he was unable to sway her. She would not come. And so he had to go alone.

# three

# feasting, fun

Hugo Kerenyi threw open the front door well before the Pinckneys rang the doorbell, and stood, half inside, half out, the cold wind rumpling his gray hair and whipping his dark-green wool necktie around his face, and billowing out the coat of his suit.

"Welcome. Welcome, dear old friends," he called. "Be careful on the steps, Everett. I'm sure there's no ice, but be careful anyway. If you must fall, please do so after dinner on your way out, when it won't mean changing the table." He brushed at the tie, which had caught on his ear. "I shouldn't have said that, should I? It might bring bad luck."

"Not for me," Everett Pinckney said. He climbed the front stoop, laboriously bracing the tip of his cane at the joints between the stones of the steps. "I've got my blue bead in my pocket. See?" He pulled off a glove, reached in, and held up a round ceramic bead, a little darker than a robin's egg.

"We Magyars left those Oriental amulets behind us centuries ago," Hugo said. He bear-hugged the short, round man, dissolving the hug into a violent shaking of Pinckney's free left hand with both of his own. "How ironic that they linger on caressed between the fingers of an illuminato."

"So that's what he is!" Mrs. Pinckney, who was a pace behind her husband, was taller for a woman than he was for a man, and made shapeless by the sheepskin coat she was wrapped up in, suede side out and collar turned up, from whose sleeves protruded her red wrists and mittened hands. Her long, pointed nose was as red as her wrists, and her eyes, which were large and round and a little popping, glistened with the cold. "You have on a new suit, don't you? I call that a bold tweed. It makes you look younger." She aimed her head right at Hugo and they kissed, coming together as squarely as a pair of contending animals.

"At last!" Hugo cried. "The Pinckneys are here and I've kissed Coral. It's really Christmas now."

As he was taking her coat, Mrs. Pinckney turned her head as far around as she could and whispered, "How is it going?"

Hugo stopped, leaving one of her arms still entrapped up to the elbow, the other one already free. His voice dropped to a murmur, and he looked toward the stairs. "Coral, I don't know. She didn't come down to open presents with us this morning." He let that failure make its impression. "But it may be going better than I think. Very likely it is."

"Keep pulling, man," Coral said, thrashing her captive arm. "There." She turned to look him in the face. "Huh. You have that funny look around the gills, now I see you better, like a fish that isn't quite fresh. I suspect it's going worse than you've let on." She rubbed the fingers of her right hand with those of her left. "I don't have presents for everybody, so I didn't bring in yours and Miriam's. I took them around to the kitchen door and left them with Mrs. Vendredy."

"Understood. Miriam didn't buy anything of her own this year." Hugo and Coral exchanged a communication of the eyes. "Presents certainly don't matter. I can forgo all that, certainly."

He took them into the living room, where Ann was waiting for them with her children, and where they greeted young Franz and Bruce Cuttler, and then Aunt Dorcas came up to Everett Pinckney, bringing with her her friend, Hazel Glidden, just in on the train. Hazel was a spare, tight, small woman, with abrupt movements, quick to extend her hand, quicker to withdraw it, and she got it right away from Professor Pinckney, although in his easy, faintly Southern manner, he liked to linger over a woman's hand. But Coral, who came up behind the Professor and edged in front of him, held it for a while.

"I'm Coral Pinckney, this man's wife. I think they were going to call me plain Cora, but they didn't stop in time," she said, offering a joke certainly used many times before. "Now what did they say your name was?"

"Glidden," Hazel said, giving a quick tug at her hand, like a fish on a hook.

"Miss or Mrs. Glidden?"

"Does it matter?"

"Not to me, surely. I think I have heard of you. At least we heard Dorcas has a very good friend who was expected today, and that must be you, and I want to tell you how glad I am to meet you if you are the friend of Dorcas I've heard about before. We've known Aunt Dorcas for ever since. The Kerenyis are like another family to us, and I've always been jealous that she's the senior and undisputed aunt around here, because otherwise I'd surely have rated an honorary title. You're here for a real occasion, Miss Glidden: the first time we've all been together in years and years—you see how I include us in that. Now tell me, do you teach girls, too?"

"No." Hazel gave another jerk and this time got her hand free. She brought it first to her side, then moved it around behind her and sent the other around to take hold of it there, so that, standing with her feet a short distance apart, she was at perfect parade rest. "I work in a drug-store."

"A drugstore! I've never spoken to anyone before, that I

recall, who worked in a drugstore." Coral smiled. "Not this side of the counter, I mean. Is it nice work?"

Dorcas said, "She's a pharmacist. And an owner. She owns and runs the leading pharmacy in King of Prussia."

"You mean to say you count out the pills that the rest of us live on? You're the pill person in white? That's what I call a strategic profession. Better than being a doctor by a long shot—oh! what a pun. I go to ten doctors, don't I Ev'rett, but I've only got one druggist. I'll be! A lady druggist."

"And is there anything wrong with that?"

"Not at all." Coral paused a moment while she considered Hazel's astringency, her big, protruding eyes fixed on Hazel's terse little mouth. "We women surely eat most of the pills, so why shouldn't one of us count them out?" She went on to say, "Now, then, there's one person that I can see I haven't said hello to yet, and there's one I've never met. Franz. Franz, I mean your wife and your new daughter. Come along to see the baby, Ev'rett."

"I can see the baby from here," he replied, but he did as he was told, the foot of his cane causing the baby much amazement as he approached.

Coral kissed Jeanette, and then the Pinckneys were allowed to adore Victoria, who was crawling on the floor in front of the fireplace, where a fire burned hotly. After a while Coral Pinckney, speaking generally, said, "Where is Mr. Kerenyi? And Miriam?"

"Father went up to get her just as you walked in," Hugo said, arriving with the Pinckneys' Martinis. "They'll be down any minute."

"I'm glad to hear that." Coral turned to Jeanette. "She's a sweet darling baby, and now I want to go out and see the plants on the sun porch."

"I wouldn't bother," said Hugo darkly.

"It's my favorite room. Franz, you come with me." She took him by the arm to lead him away, but he seemed reluctant to go. "Now, come on. You see plenty of Victoria." She pulled him in close to her as they left the room. "I don't give a hoot about the plants," she said. "Of course, if you want to look at them, be my guest, but not me. I wanted to have a word with you. Or did you guess?" She laughed and squeezed him. "You know, you may as well learn right now that having a baby in a house can be a godsend. It's the perfect diversion. Having a baby around that everyone was looking at has given me the chance for more confidential conversations than you'd ever believe. Held practically right out in the open. Like now. Here we are. What a lot of sunshine to be in one room."

It was a pleasant room, the sun porch, with gauzy curtains pulled back and tied close to the supports between the French windows that otherwise filled all the outside walls. The furniture was all of wood, painted apple green, with little flowers stenciled on it. There were stepped-back tiers of glass shelves for plants and some marble slabs on the floor with water traps grooved around their edges for the larger pots; but there were few plants of any kind growing in the room now, just a couple of philodendrons, one or two withered chrysanthemums that must have been gifts when in flower and that had not been thrown out, and a few ugly succulents.

Coral looked around. "Lord!" she exclaimed. "Do you remember this room, Franzie, when there'd have been three hundred plants blooming in it, or anyway growing, and a thicket of ferns and palms in both corners? Just like a jungle it was, at night, and one of your mother's favorite places to see people in, and it would have had that smell— you know what I mean—that smell of slimy pot bottoms and wet tendrils. It tells you all you need to know."

"I didn't like Mother's plants. They always seemed to take so much time when it wasn't convenient."

"Nice things do. Now answer a question. How do you find it here?"

"Not all that bad. Mother doesn't seem very strong. Father doesn't seem any different. No, not really so bad at all."

"I don't believe it."

"Don't believe what?"

"That anyone as intelligent as you are, and let me just put this in, too"—Coral Pinckney reared back, her nose pointing straight at Franz, her eyes looking to him like china eggs, and terrible—"that anyone as knocked around as you were as a boy could be so insensitive. Not bad? This tragic house?"

"Tragic?" Franz repeated. "Tragic? Oh, come on."

"If you don't like tragic, find another word. Please be my guest. But that's the one I'd use. Hasn't your father talked to you?"

"Not since I got here. We haven't had a chance, really."

"No? Huh! I'd have made the chance. How long has it been since you were in this house?"

"Nearly five years."

"That's too long a time. Why haven't you been back?"

"I've been busy, Coral. Europe one year. A Guggenheim. Writing my book. New job. New baby—"

She interrupted him. "Spare me your entry in *Who's Who*. Nobody these days goes five years without seeing Mom and Pop, Franz. It's un-American."

"It happened that way."

"Nothing ever does that, either. You've been criticized for it—for not trying to help things along here—by a lot of your father's and mother's old friends, who know how you were the apple of his eye for so long. And you're the son of the house—a big responsibility when things start to crack up. I've defended you, considering all that's happened since, but if you come and go and leave things the same, I don't know what I'll say—or think. Not that you'd care about that, necessarily. Still, the academic world is a small one."

She strolled a few feet down the room toward the other end and the other doors, but she turned on him again. "Let me just ask you this: how would you deal with a divorce?"

"A divorce! Are you serious? Have they said something?"

"Of course I'm serious. Children always think their own parents are divorceproof. Many a child's found out the truth about that. When a man groans as much as your father has been groaning the last few months, anything could happen. Your mother doesn't seem to care about anything enough to do it, but he's hurting, Franz."

"I don't believe that will happen. What would they do?"

"Well you might ask. All Princeton is waiting for it to be announced. Call anyone you know around here and ask them. You'll soon find out that the situation at the Kerenyis'—and I'm sick to death of that phrase; I hear it all the time: the situation at the Kerenyis'—it's on everybody's mind and they're always after me to tell them about it because of our being the oldest and best friends—it's universally regarded as an emergency and a disaster. Just check with some of them. Be my guest, because it would be a relief to me to be on vacation for a day." She'd walked on again, Franz tagging along behind now. "I'm stating facts, not gossip. And I happen to think—"

She stopped abruptly. She had reached the other French doors, the ones at the front end, from which there was a clear view across the living room into the front hall. "Lord, there's your grandfather, and he's all alone. All alone," she said. "Come along. We mustn't miss this." She hurried out.

Mr. Kerenyi walked slowly from the hall into the living room and stopped in the middle of the front end, ten feet from the tree. All voices in the room stopped, too, one by one, as everybody realized he had entered by himself.

Hugo came forward. "Where is Miriam, my wife?"

Mr. Kerenyi looked at his son and slowly shook his

head. "She will not join us. She said she would, and I waited, but then she changed her mind. I could not get her to change it back again."

"What reason did she give?"

"Only that she couldn't."

"Couldn't!" Hugo laughed sarcastically. "And you, all of you who spoke to her this morning, can you perhaps explain it any better?"

Franz shook his head, Dorcas was silent, Jeanette turned aside, Bruce shrugged his shoulders. Ann said, "She told me that she'd grown to dislike crowds."

Hugo spread wide his hands. "This? A crowd?"

"Father, let us not discuss it like this. Just leave it as Grandfather did: she's changed her mind."

Hugo got loud. "I've heard that word from her, too: 'change.' Yes, I've heard it, too. Let me tell you, it's a two-edged sword. Well, so be it," he said slowly.

"Let me go up and talk to her," suggested Coral.

"No. So be it. We've tried all that. We sent her breakfast up. Ann wanted to. It was against my better judgment. There is no reason to play along with her any further. This is a turning point, I am telling you all that. This is a real turning point. Not coming to Christmas dinner with her family." He was very severe, but not angry.

"It's inexcusable," said Aunt Dorcas. "I am very offended."

"Yes," Hugo said. "But so be it. So be it. And furthermore, henceforth this situation will all be brought out in the open. I do not intend to pretend about it any more. She has no lingering symptoms from her illness; this is a new pathology. Henceforth we will all speak freely of Miriam's condition. I know of no better word for it, although I can think of others I would personally prefer to use. *Let it see the light!*" he suddenly shouted.

And then, it seemed just as they watched, something happened to him, something he perhaps willed into being. "Back to cocktails, everybody," he called out, and his voice was almost cheerful. "We will not let this spoil our Christmas. No, by God. We will carry on the family traditions without her. We *shall* be merry, by God. By ourselves. Bicycle wheels will go around without your grandmother, Billy; and what's one person more or less to play with a doll house, Lucy? Drink your cocktails, everybody, and we'll all have another, as many as we can guzzle down, before Mrs. Vendredy comes to summon us." He rubbed his hands and smiled. "I, for one, intend to get three if I can, and I intend to feast, and then we'll all go down to the lake and go ice skating and have lots of fun at it, too. I haven't been ice skating with my family in years, and nothing, nobody, is going to spoil my fun. Father, what would you like for an *apéritif?* Everybody start in to talk again. Those are my orders."

And everybody did. They talked and laughed and tried to cover over the fact that there was now, apparently, a real situation at the Kerenyis'. Then Mrs. Vendredy came in in her apron, carrying a huge wooden spoon, made for stirring up soup for a regiment, which she held, Hugo pointed out, as a herald might a trumpet, and announced that dinner was served. But—

"Where is Mrs. Kerenyi?" she asked, her long, narrow face, that so belied the idea that all cooks are fat and jolly, going even more glum.

"There is only one Mrs. Kerenyi for dinner, and that is she," Hugo said, pointing to Jeanette.

Mrs. Vendredy looked at him, then at Mrs. Pinckney, then at Ann, and to Ann said, before she left, "I'd sooner have dropped the goose, pan, grease, and all, on the kitchen floor, than to have this happen."

"Come while it's hot, come while it's hot, as they say in lesser places," Hugo said. He moved around the room, urging each of them in turn, a collie amongst sheep. When he got to Aunt Dorcas he plucked her buttony sleeve and leaned down to say into her ear, "It is really so nice to have Hazel in the house at last." To which Aunt Dorcas

replied that she wouldn't be back soon if anyone else con-
descended to her the way Coral Pinckney had. "Oh, come
now," he said, laughing, as if at an absurdity. "Don't let
her pay any attention to that." Then he hurried forward to
walk beside Ann, and whispered to her that Aunt Dorcas
was cooking up one of her scenes, and to be nice to her
and little Miss Glidden, because she, Ann, was now to be
hostess at the table. He then went on ahead and took the
extra place setting away and put it on the buffet, very os-
tentatiously, as the rest of them came into the dining
room, so that they noticed. He bowed to it, said, "I'll lay it
to rest," and crossed the knives, forks, and spoons carefully over the plate and dropped the napkin over the lot,
then tipped an imaginary hat, as if in reverential farewell,
turned, and told everybody to "Adjust, adjust," and close
up the empty space at table. Indeed, he acted as if nothing
was bothering him any more, as if nothing could. Everyone who'd been there the night before got the same impression: he seemed in far more genuine good spirits
today, not forcing them at all, his enjoyment so convincing
that it was hard to believe he could be acting.

For dinner there was green turtle soup, and then both a
turkey and the goose, and to go with them a mixture of
traditional American and Central European dishes, rang-
ing from red cabbage done with lots of onion and caraway
seed to mashed potatoes. This time the wines were
French, a choice of Beaunes, red or white, in case anybody
preferred the latter with turkey; but Hugo did not allow
anybody who took cranberries to have anything other than
sweet apple cider, which meant that Mrs. Vendredy's
cranberries went really only to the Cuttler children and to
Hazel Glidden, who didn't drink. Dessert was banana ice
cream that Mrs. Vendredy had made and brought over,
and mincemeat and apple pies, done in the American
manner, and then there were nuts to be cracked and eaten
at the table with some Emmentaler, if anyone wanted it by

that time, and for this Hugo brought out port, "not vintage, but not bad all the same."

When Coral tasted it she cried, "Not bad! It's *good*. My Lord, Hugo, when I think of all the dismal things you've had to eat and drink in our house this winter, night after night after night!" She glanced at Ann and Franz, significantly. Then she turned to the old man on her left and explained, "I just go to the liquor store and ask them what they have by the gallon that goes with frozen carrots and peas, Mr. Kerenyi."

He said, "One used to buy by the cask; why not by the gallon?"

"I'll have you to dinner and then you will know."

"The company was good, and wine is wine," Hugo said.

"Barely, barely," said Professor Pinckney, looking through his glass at a light.

Hugo said, "In wine, as in everything else, our times are going to force us to do new things, and do them in new ways. I think that perhaps it's a good thing. The capacity to adapt is certainly the most attractive quality of youth. Let us steal it and keep it ourselves."

"You were talking very differently last night, Hugo," Bruce Cuttler put in. He turned to Professor Pinckney. "Last night he was boasting that he had made time stand still—with a certain amount of help from the rest of us."

"The King Canute of the fourth dimension?" Pinckney suggested.

"It is said, Bruce, that I always want everything, and certainly I want both the past and the present, and what is more I'll get them. But I have a question for my esteemed colleague, the Dunstable Professor of Islamic Literature, et cetera, et cetera. It is this: if a man, at the age of sixty or so, where both you and I now find ourselves, Everett, is given the choice of either continuing along the way he has been coming for many years, or of changing that way, which ought he to do?"

Pinckney said, "What a question to ask a man at

Christmas dinner. If I'd have known about it in advance, I'd have stayed as sober as Miss Glidden."

Hazel Glidden, as one of her only heard utterances, said, "Why I do it. Why I do it."

"I won't let you turn it, Everett. I am too serious for that."

"Why then, I'd say that the average man will continue the way he has come, and probably should."

"I think that won't do. Because it can only mean a winding down."

"Or a winding up."

"Not after sixty. No. He should change directions. That is the road of juvenescence. Continuing vitality. Of life itself. To go on to new things, with new gusto and enthusiasm. Those are the qualities that distinguish the man who never stops, who accomplishes to the end, from the one who empties too soon, like a half-filled glass. I, for one, look forward, like my Goethe, even more like Beethoven and Rembrandt, to a late style, and maybe a couple of them."

"Hugo, that strikes me as superficial," his father said.

"Then that is because I have stated it badly. Or because you find profound, wisdom which is more resigned. December wisdom."

"Late styles are usually full of it. Nor are they acts of choice."

"Well, I'm going to spend my autumn south of the Equator, figuratively speaking, where it's spring." Hugo raised his glass of port and toasted without rising. "To sudden changes and quick decisions, to ninety-degree angles, to new things to think about and do, new ideas, new books, new pens and clean paper, even to new suits like this dumfounding one I have on today for the first time—don't deny it, for I looked at myself in the mirror and it cannot be denied that it dominates the landscape—and to all people whose instinct is to keep moving and say yes. There. How's that for a toast?"

Professor Pinckney asked dryly, "What practical effects may we anticipate?"

"Well, for one, I'm going to change my field."

"You're fooling," Franz said, very shocked.

"Hugo, don't tell me you're going to join me in the Middle East. No," said Pinckney.

"No, not that. But I've had enough of the Enlightenment."

"Has the Enlightenment had enough of you?" Franz said. "If I may strike the hammer of metaphor upon the anvil of reification . . ."

"It must get along without me."

"Where will you go then?"

"Probably back to the sixteenth century."

"From Goethe to Martin Luther. That is, indeed, jumping backward," Mr. Kerenyi observed.

"Well, I've said what I set out to say. And, as I look around me, I realize that dinner is over. Ann, if you please . . ." He waited for her to stand up.

She did so. And then everyone else did.

"It certainly was delicious," Jeanette said. "I think it's the first time I ever tasted roast goose."

"So now you know about that, too," said her husband.

Out in the hallway, Hugo insisted on separating the ladies from the gentlemen, in order to take the latter with him back to the library for coffee and brandy, while the former, he said, would also be given coffee for themselves in the small room just forward of the dining room. "I don't know whether it's accepted practice for the sexes to divide when dinner is at midday, but in the eighteenth century they separated at every possible opportunity, so we'll use that procedure. I'm not suggesting a reformation of that as yet. Ann, take your gender along."

The division of the party gave Ann the opportunity to talk to Coral Pinckney, although their exchanges could be only discontinuous, broken by frequent interruptions. Still, each of them made points. It began when Dorcas and

Hazel were still upstairs, powdering in Dorcas's room, while Jeanette was off in the back room with Victoria, and the Cuttler children were in the kitchen with Mrs. Vendredy.

"Well?" Coral asked.

"It's terrible, Coral. I don't know what to say."

"I'm glad you realize it. Franz won't."

"Or doesn't dare to."

Coral, seeing the expression on Ann's face, put her arms around her. "My poor Annie. My poor little Annie. I know. And you can't come running over to my house to cry about this the way you used to. That's what's terrible."

"And the way he was just now at dinner," Ann said.

At that point Dorcas came downstairs, and the Cuttler children appeared from the kitchen. After asking them about school, and thus getting them turned over to Dorcas, Coral whispered another aside.

"Have you thought what it means, to a man like your father, to find himself superfluous where he should be most needed?"

"I know how I'd feel."

"For a man like your father to stop counting is intolerable. You've got to remember that if you want to be fair."

"Do you take his side, then?"

"I'll take the side of the loser, and don't you be too sure who that's going to be."

"That's the most sensible thought yet."

Hazel came into the room, and Ann got her coffee and made a little fuss over her before adding her to Dorcas and the children. Then she got back to Coral.

"Bruce thinks that maybe Mother has simply grown to dislike him. That awful word they use now: incompatibility. That is what's at the bottom of all her strangeness. Mother's own eccentric version of how to treat incompatibility. Could that be it?"

"It wouldn't be hard. Shall I tell you something? I once came near to loving your father, years ago. If he'd asked me, I might have—" Coral had to stop when Lucy came to ask her mother why they weren't getting ready for the ice skating. They shooed her away. "Might have met him somewhere—you know what I mean. Maybe more than once, too, depending on how it went. The rest of us, all of Miriam's women friends, always thought he must be terrific at making love. He flirted with us, yet so far as I know he never did anything more. I'd have heard. And the two of them gave that feeling people do—of having a real sex life, and going right on with it when for the rest of us . . . well . . ."

"I never think of them that way."

"I should hope not. He was stunning, just stunning. Lord." Coral breathed in slowly, rolling her round eyes very comically. "He's still not bad, for a man of sixty. Vigorous. I wonder about— Anyway, I still have special feelings for him. But sometimes I dislike him, too, and I'm not even a member of his family. He's just too much, isn't he? And perhaps if I were Miriam I'd have grown tired of him and come to dislike him so that I'd be willing to get rid of everything else, Annie, to be rid of him. Maybe. Maybe. That's what it would have come down to."

Jeanette came into the room, and Ann got her coffee. Ann noticed, from the distance of much of the house, that the lowest string of lights on the tree in the main living room had gone out, and she took Coral there to help her find the dead bulb that was spoiling the series, and replace it.

"It's been a small local scandal," Coral said. "I tried to tell Franz that. She won't have anything to do with him. She won't eat with him—sneaks down when he's out, or in the middle of the night. Mrs. Vendredy does what she can for both of them, but if it weren't for us, he'd be half starved."

"I do appreciate that, Coral."

"Don't bother to thank me. We're glad to have him to dinner. Ev'rett has the capacity many of your father's colleagues do not, to turn off his mind when Hugo is taking too long to say something or is being, you know, too ornate, and yet turn it back on when Hugo finally gets to the point, so he can reply. He can converse with Hugo, whereas a lot of people can only interject. Sometimes I leave the room. He isn't likely to notice, unless of course we're all alone. Thirty-odd years of that? I don't wonder Miriam hates him."

"That wasn't what we said."

"No, you're right. There! You've found it." The lights went on when Ann put a new one in one of the sockets. "Give me the dud and I'll toss it in the wastebasket." Coral did so and returned to Ann, beside the tree. "She's chosen a way to escape from him calculated to hurt and hurt and hurt."

"That would seem to be the idea, but I don't think it will work that way."

" 'Will' maybe not, but 'has,' yes. Annie, if he should go out of her life, whatever will happen to your poor mother? She'll be around your neck, I'm afraid. I don't see how, the way she is, she could take care of herself indefinitely. Oh, maybe she'd make a comeback if she had to. But I doubt it. There's more wrong with her than just Hugo, surely, though he may have started it all. They were such a team in the old days; I still think they need each other. He's beginning to seem just a little old-fashioned, you know. Ev'rett tells me plenty of people think that about him, and not just the Young Turk demographical lot like Franz, either. You know the way he can rumble on about humanistic values and the universal man. Well, those things are old hat now. As bad as genealogies. Ev'rett calls it all periwig-history. Times change, but not your father, no matter what he says. He'll have Luther talking like Goethe before he's through, you'll see. He's going to feel more and more out of things, Ev'rett thinks. And with his vanity, he'll notice when the students yawn—or snicker. You've got to try to wire them back together if you can, you and

Franz, because he may face disappointments he doesn't imagine. Bad as their sticking together might be, it's better than nothing. I'm not fooling. As far as I'm concerned, that's what this holiday is all about: wiring them back together."

Ann looked evenly at her. "That, more or less, was what I thought Father wanted, Coral, but I'm not so sure. I'm wondering more and more just exactly what it was he did have in mind when he planned this Christmas."

Coral stared at her in surmise. "Well, now . . ."

Another interruption, this time Mrs. Vendredy wanting some instructions on what to do with leftovers, and Ann went to see if Dorcas and Hazel wanted to take some back to Pennsylvania with them. It was only just before the men reappeared that Ann got to Coral for a final question.

"Tell me, what do you think of Monique? The girl who lives here."

"He's been taking her to all the concerts, I know that. Last time, when the Amadeus were doing those in-between Beethoven quartets with the Slavic name, I discovered he hadn't even told Miriam about it. He didn't give her the chance to turn him down, he just went ahead and took the girl on her ticket."

"Mother seems so fond of her."

"That's happened before in these cases."

"It would certainly cheapen what I now think of as very sad events."

"Ev'rett's put his finger on that. He's very upset about it. He said, what if behind the grand Kerenyi façade there turns out to be a motel. I asked Leo Barton what he thought of her—she's a student of his. He said she was bright and ingratiating. Now, you have to believe me, I didn't say a word to lead him into his next remark. He went on to say that she was a real beauty, too. And he sort of made a funny face at me, and it wasn't his stroke that affected the right side of his face, if you're thinking that."

"I didn't know about it."

"Well, he did it, and he said, 'I might add that Glo'—that's his wife—'Glo certainly wouldn't let her live in *our* house.'"

"I wish she had," Ann said.

Coral asked, "Just what *do* you think your father had in mind when he planned this Christmas?"

"Maybe just exactly what's happened," Ann replied.

There were sounds from the library. Coral said, "Here comes Ev'rett. Thank the Lord he can't skate, because that means I don't have to, either."

The next stage of the Kerenyi Christmas was about to begin.

Hugo came toward the front hall shouting through his cupped hands, "Halloa! Halloa!" and turning his head. "All skaters come forward. All skaters assemble." In a short time everyone, willingly or not, except Miriam and old Mr. Kerenyi, was there. Hugo had found the stock of old ice skates in the attic and got them down and piled them under the front stairs, along with extra socks, some long wool scarves, old stocking caps, and a couple of pairs of knitted mittens. "Come on. Find your own or something that will fit you. If you don't find something exactly right, take a pair that's too large and an extra pair of socks will do it. Come on, everybody, find what you need. We never gave any skates away and we could outfit a family twice this size. Franz, that pair there was yours until just yesterday, it seems to me, and Ann, something happened to yours, just to prove my rule by an exception, but you used to be able to wear your mother's shoes, so you ought to be able to wear her skates. These." He disentangled a pair of high black boots and gleaming blades. "Almost new, you see, and very good ones. Off with your shoes, Aunt Dorcas, and try on these, or these. And now, Hazel Glidden, let me help you. Here, let me measure your foot."

"I don't know how to skate, Professor Kerenyi," Miss Glidden said.

"That doesn't matter. Who ever was born with knowledge? The important thing is to be open to its acquisition. We are a skating family, and you have officially joined us today, as Aunt Dorcas's protégée. So skate you must."

"But I can't."

He paid no attention, but reached for her foot, down on his knees in front of her by the pile of skates.

"Really, Mr. Kerenyi," she said. She twitched her right foot out of his reach, only to have him take her left. "I think I'd be afraid, never having skated as a child. And I'm afraid of falling."

"Dropping things, too," Aunt Dorcas put in. "She is, Hugo. Still . . ." There was perhaps just the hint of disdain in Aunt Dorcas's voice. "Well, I suppose that is one of the advantages of a New England childhood. We had our winters."

"Don't let Aunt Dorcas get away with being so superior, Hazel Glidden. Come on. Women who are competent in one thing are competent in all things." He had her foot and put his ruler alongside it, noted the length, and began to scuffle around amongst the skates. "Damn. Did I cut my finger? No. Or just a little. Anyway, never give in to fears, either. We'll take you a pair . . ." He untangled one whose laces, tied together, had got wrapped around the blades of another pair. "We'll just take you this pair in case you change your mind when you see the fun." He stood up. "Carry them with you. You'll catch the itch from holding them." He watched while Miss Glidden examined them to see how they were put together. She tested the width of the blades. "Narrow, eh? But think of a bicycle tire. The secret of balance is in movement. Nor are our feet all that big, considering what happens above them—especially in my case. Let's see, everybody. . . . They don't let you skate on the canal anywhere any more if they can stop you, so the question is where we should go on the lake. How about up beyond the boathouse? Which leaves the question of the cars. I think it makes sense for you to

take your station wagon, Bruce. You can get the most people in it. And Coral and Everett can take their car because
they may want to leave early. So everything's decided."

The big station wagon pulled out of the driveway first,
and was followed by the Pinckneys' Hillman, Coral at the
wheel, Everett Pinckney beside her in front, and Franz
Kerenyi in back by himself. There was scarcely enough
time for Coral to exhort Franz to make himself master of
the situation in his father's house lest it become master of
him, and Professor Pinckney to remark mildly that he
thought it was only very marginally any of her business,
and what good was advice that couldn't be followed, before they were down at the lakeside. She parked and got
out of the car and tipped her seat forward so that Franz
could get out of the back, while her husband pulled himself, laboriously because of his arthritis and his cane, out
of his side. The Cuttlers' station wagon was already
parked and unloaded, its passengers moving faster. They
walked from the road over to the edge of the ice, where a
few other people were sitting or putting on or removing
skates. There were a number of other skaters out, and their
figures could be seen weaving across toward the other
bank, and over in front of the boathouse, and down toward
the bridge, and off to the right toward the narrows and
then Stoneybrook, whose banks had a cover of trees and
brush made up of a dense understory of bushes out of
which rose high old trees of the rather mongrel shapes of
those varieties that thrive in flood plains. As the Pinckneys, nonskaters, and Franz, who most inevitably was
going to skate, approached, they could hear Hugo happily
calling to somebody he knew on the ice, and his arms were
never still from gesturing or waving, except to put a lace
rapidly through an eye.

"Hurry up, Franz," he shouted. "Hazel Glidden is holding out for the time being; she wants to watch us for a
while and then see, but she'll certainly change her mind
when she sees you and me race, and especially when she

sees Billy and Lucy scoot off. Watch the signs, children, or anyway stay within the approved zones, meaning close in here, and don't go up near there where the moving water comes in. That is an absolutely solemn grandpaternal command. You'll watch them, won't you, Ann? You must keep an eye on them."

"Of course," Ann said abruptly, embarrassed to realize that she had glanced at her brother.

"And Bruce, you give Jeanette the keys to your car so she can run the heater and warm up if Victoria gets cold— who I must say right now looks like nothing so much as a giant slug all wrapped in pastry and ready to be deep fried. I'll spell you holding her, Jeanette, if nobody else will and you change your mind and want to join us, which I hope will be the case, because you must be better at it than anyone else, being a real Borealite. So, now I am off. Don't get cold, Hazel Glidden. Don't be timid, Lucy; it's a bad habit to get into. Just strike on out and fall down if you must. Billy, one of the secrets of skating on figure blades, in case you don't know, is to sit on your heels. Like this, see? With your knees a little bent and limber. So. Otherwise those ratchets up front will catch in the ice and you'll go sprawling. I'm off, the first one on the ice—as always."

He had side-stepped his way down the shallow bank, and with a series of powerful pushes, he sped out over the ice, dodging anyone who was in his way, wheeling sideways to come to fast stops when he wanted to turn, as he did about every hundred feet, to wave to his family back on the bank. Ann and the children got out on the ice next, she holding each of them by one hand; they skated in Illinois and were by no means so new at it as Hugo seemed to want to think them, as if only near him could anyone in his family learn any lusty, strenuous activity. Bruce Cuttler, who had been reared in the District of Columbia, where the possibility of ice skating was not so common, but who had done some when he'd lived with the Kerenyis, got out on the ice next, tentatively and carefully, and after a while was moving about with his usual assurance. Dorcas and Hazel, with Jeanette, and Franz at a distance, and then, close to their own car, the Pinckneys, were still on the bank.

Dorcas said, as she was about to leave, "You should go to the Cuttlers' car, too, if you get cold, Hazel. Don't stand there and take a chill."

"Dorcas, I do not need you to warn me not to lose too much body heat." Hazel lowered her voice. "I think it would make me nauseous, that side-to-side skating motion, this soon after that meal. That's why I'm waiting." She let Dorcas go, then said to Jeanette, whom she'd picked out as a friend at the table, "I think you agree with me, don't you, Mrs. Kerenyi? I saw you picking at that goose meat as if it was spoiled. I can't wait, myself, for an hour's peace and quiet and a glass of buttermilk. Dorcas feels the same way."

Jeanette nodded. "It's the European in them," she explained.

"Well, don't let your husband ruin your stomach," Miss Glidden advised. "Or hers, either." And she moved in close to look at the minute oval of face which was all that was exposed of diminutive Victoria.

"I'm not going to do things the Kerenyi way, at the dinner table or away from it."

"Good for you," Hazel said.

Hugo sailed up to them but went by. "Come on, Franz," he called. "I'll race you now." He waited while Franz finished lacing his boots and came onto the ice, then he grabbed his son's hand and pulled him a little distance. "Before we race, though, what do you think? You've seen now just what your mother is like." Hugo picked up speed.

Franz stroked along doggedly. "Yes."

"I hope you agree with my position. There are too many things in life like this"—Hugo pushed mightily with his left leg, turned a right figure three, then another, leaving a trilobed mark in the ice, and cut in close again to Franz's side—"to give out before you have to. It's not for me. No, it isn't." He sped ahead again and again came back; Franz continued to go forward at his own speed. "I see you don't get onto ice very often in California. But I hear they have lots of artificial rinks, so a person could keep it up if he wanted to." He was away again, and came back this time only long enough to say, "I'm going to give you a while to get your legs. Can you still do your proper figure eights on your outer and inner edges? You'd better be able to. What good does it do a man to know all about the latrines at Ellis Island if he can't do a neat figure eight?"

Hugo returned once more to the bank, went past Miss Glidden and Jeanette, and stopped to speak to the Pinckneys privately. "It is a sad day, my good friends," he said. "And yet a glorious one. The things that matter continue. The earth rolls, the wind blows clean, the sun shines still. Imagine skating on natural ice on Christmas Day in this climate. Wonderful. Now don't get cold and don't get bored. Leave when you feel like it. And I will be around to see you tomorrow or the next day, for there are going to be a good many things for us to discuss."

Coral started to say something, but the generally retiring Everett talked her down. "Come when you wish, Hugo, naturally. You can continue to count on us."

Hugo came up off the ice and took one of their hands in each of his. "Thank God," he said. He started back for the ice, but remembered Aunt Dorcas's remarks before dinner. "And Coral, if you get the chance, you might make a special effort to be nice to that funny little Glidden woman. She's a quivering sensibility, it seems, and feels out of things."

Off he went again, this time to find Bruce and tell him to go and relieve Ann of the children so that she could skate a little bit with her father. Bruce did so, and soon Hugo and

Ann were proceeding at a more stately pace up toward the brook, but not too far, their hands interlocked in front and behind. Hugo hummed a waltz, and they kept time.

After a while he said, "I'm sorry about the way things have gone. But we mustn't let that spoil our pleasure. We have given her the chance." He slowed down so he could look sideways at his daughter. "And I do want to say one thing to you I didn't want to say in front of the others. Don't forget this one thing: the cutting herself off that your mother's doing—it isn't just impersonal, and it isn't just personal, either, just affecting herself, all involved with private problems only. It's got a target. I'm it. I don't like the position. I'm the target and I don't like it."

"Perhaps less than you think," Ann said.

"Perhaps more than you'll grant."

He stopped for his handkerchief and wiped the tears from the cold away from his eyes. "The cold makes you look as if you were made of a dozen flavors of Bavarian cream, Annie. I guess we should turn back. I want to skate with the children before it gets too late. But I did want to say that to you, what I just said, before any more time had passed."

Ann sought out her brother and asked him to skate with her. They went along, skimming slowly over the ice, neither of them wanting to go fast, just staying in step with each other, he only a very little bit taller than she, looking almost like two adolescents together with their stocking caps pulled down over their ears—a younger brother-and-sister pair. They talked about their lives, their families—distantly, objectively. They had never been very close. Then Ann brought up, as she had inevitably to do, the subject of Miriam and Hugo.

"I suppose we're going to have to talk about the situation here, but I don't really want to. I'm tired of it, and it's so—knotty. Or knotted."

"Who isn't tired of it?"

"Think how tired they must be of it," Ann said.

"Then they shouldn't have got themselves into it."

"You don't always realize that when you start something, Franzie. What are your ideas about it? Coral tells me you said it didn't seem to you to be too bad. I don't believe that."

"I didn't want to gossip with her. Of course it's bad. But I'll tell you, I don't know how bad it is, and I really don't care. Ann, all I want to do is just get away from here tomorrow, and get through visiting Jeanette's parents up in Ithaca and seeing the people I worked with at Cornell, and then get back to Palo Alto."

"Running from it."

"Don't try to needle me with that one," he said.

They circled around the far end of the designated skating area. Ann said, "You have to worry about it, Franz. And so do I."

"Why?"

"Self-interest."

"Running is better self-interest."

"I think our only hope is to persuade Father to stick it out for a while longer. Maybe he will anyway, but get him to promise. Just ask him that, as his children. Gang up on him to ask him that much. Maybe something will happen with time. Otherwise we're going to be worrying a lot more about them."

"You haven't been listening to what I've said, Annie. Not me. *Not me!* I live a long way off, and as of this holiday, I've decided to stay there, too. I'm me and where I am, and they're them, and they're here. Jeanette says she'll never come to this house and town again—so that's the impression they've made on her. I stand with her."

Ann said quietly, "What will I do? What will *I* do? You're the only person I can turn to. Bruce is so cynical about them, doesn't like them at all, really, and they certainly feel the same way."

"That's Father and his damned snobbery. There are no bigger snobs than priests and old-fashioned professors, you know that."

"Mother, too. Almost more. And it's gone on and on. I can't completely blame them."

"Why not?"

She glanced at him. "Don't you know?"

"Know what?"

"Oh," she said. "Oh."

He slowed down and stopped and turned to her. "I don't want to hear some depressing revelation, Annie. I'm not up to it this afternoon."

"I don't think you'll consider it that. But I think you ought to know. I don't think it should be a secret between you and me, because it will come out one day. And you should know they have points on their side—and not just about Bruce and me. When Bruce and I realized that we ought to consider getting married—you understand?"

"Yes."

"It was late March. He had the term to finish out as an assistant, teaching something in the Economics department. Working on his own thing, too. Anyway, he couldn't leave. But we talked it over and decided that he should see Father and make a bargain with him. Bruce had decided to go to Chicago to work, and he was sure he could turn a small nest egg, if he could get one, into a lot of money, and he has. I went along with it. It seemed reasonable to me. I stayed in the background, though, because Bruce didn't want them to know I'd helped him figure it out, just in case they balked and it all went wrong. We might have got married anyway, but we might not have. We were in love, but neither one of us thought that necessarily had to lead to marriage—and if it didn't, he didn't want me to be on the outs with them. I'd need them, obviously. So he went to Father and presented his terms. It wasn't so much—about thirty-five thousand dollars in cash and a good allowance for me for three years—we didn't need all that, actually. Father had a fit, as you can imagine. Roared about blackmail and blackguards. Mother was worse, because of the idea of putting a price on a wedding, just to save appearances, she thought, and she was terribly worried about me. They gave in, though. Almost had to." Ann smiled. "Because otherwise they'd have been put in the position of putting more value on money than Bruce did. So we got married and came back and lived in the house while Bruce finished out the term, and then we went away. You must know that part, because it was about that time you came back from England."

Franz gave his quick laugh. "Jesus Christ."

"You never knew any of this?"

"Never anything but what I could see for myself."

"It shows you how they hated it."

Franz said, "Neither of us has exactly been what they wanted, have we?"

"Or married it, either. No. It wasn't too pleasant living in the house for those weeks, but it was the only thing to do. We kept out of each other's ways, thanks to the back stairs. And eating off trays. And Father came around, sort of. He didn't grow to like Bruce, but he came around. You remember the beautiful necklace I had on last night? He had it made for me, and gave it to me when we left. It's made out of some enamel strips that came off a reliquary, I think. I think Gothic, maybe fourteenth century. Austrian, or even Hungarian. He had the strips cut into pieces and set in gold. It fits me, goes with me. It was a considerate present, if you know what I mean."

"Remarkably, for him."

"Mother was different. She thought it was all so squalid and undignified. She was in the midst of menopause and was pretty tense anyway. She didn't forgive it. Father found a soothing way out, too. Can you guess?" Franz shook his head. "He began to refer to the bargain as a dowry. That made it all right. It had a proper, old-fashioned, acceptable sound to it. Whereas she referred

139

more than once to Bruce as my 'cash-and-carry husband.'"

They skated slowly back toward the bank. "So that's why I don't hold their feelings about Bruce too much against them. It was hard for them. And I certainly haven't wanted to lose them because of it. I don't want to lose them now. I just feel that the best hope is to try to keep the situation static for as long as we can. Mother just might come out of her slump, if you want to call it that. Try to help."

Franz said, "I don't think anything I can say will help."

"But if you see a chance, try."

"All right, if I see a chance, I will. Just to keep them off my back."

"And Franz. Needless to say, the settlement, the thirty-five thousand, will be taken care of in their wills, or Grandfather's, somehow. I mean, you'll get more. That was part of the understanding. So you don't need to worry about that. I remember how you were about our allowances when we were kids."

"Annie," he replied, "that is now the least of my worries, and if you don't understand that, you don't understand the slightest thing about me."

"Right now the least, maybe; but sooner or later you'd have got around to that question. I know you."

The Pinckneys did get cold and decided they would go home, so they went to say good-by to the other spectators in their party, Miss Glidden and Jeanette, and to offer to take either or both of them along. Everett went to the Cutler car where Jeanette was sitting, but she did not feel she should leave. Neither did Miss Glidden, so long as Aunt Dorcas was still out on the ice. Coral, who'd gone to ask her, tried to be friendly.

"I have a sister I sometimes go to visit in Harrisburg. Perhaps one day you and Dorcas and I might have lunch together when I'm on my way through."

Hazel unbent a bit. "That might be nice, if I'm not on duty."

"The Kerenyis are so precious to me, Dorcas's sister is like my own. I'm so worried now, I'm really not myself. I do talk on and on, but I mean well."

"Perhaps it will all turn out all right."

"It won't be easy for Dorcas if it doesn't."

"No."

"She's connected with a strange family," Coral said. "Just look at them out there. Ann and Franz and Hugo. Fascinating, the whole lot of them, though sometimes easier to love than to like."

Miss Glidden nodded.

"Hugo hasn't made Franz race with him yet. I don't want to have to watch it."

Miss Glidden looked quickly sideways at her.

"Too much like painful old times. I'm rather surprised that Hugo brought everybody down here. It's not a place with very pleasant associations for them."

Miss Glidden nibbled at the bait. "Why not? Professor Kerenyi seems to love it."

"It was right over there, right up toward that bend in the bank, where the trees are half in the water, old stumps and snags and all, that they found the other little boy."

"Other little boy?"

"The other child. You know about him? The one called Nicky."

"Well, no, I don't."

"One of the strange things about the story is that they always say he died of exposure. I suppose in a sense he did. They won't ever use the other word."

"Which is?"

"Drowning."

"Oh." Miss Glidden looked severely at Coral. "Dorcas has never mentioned it."

"They rarely do. That's because of Franz, I think. The

little boy was with him. A winter day just like this, just
about this time in the afternoon, almost darkening. He
didn't keep close enough track on him and Nicholas
strayed off. By the time Franz, who was playing hockey or
something with his own friends, missed him, it was dark,
and they couldn't find him. He'd gone up toward the brook
where he wasn't supposed to be, but he was too little to
pay much attention to that, and very spoiled, too, and he'd
gone through where the ice wasn't firm. Behind a fallen
log, which was why they couldn't find him. Actually, when
they did, finally, his head was out of the water. You
know. He'd almost, not quite, drowned. He had water in
his lungs, but still, it was not quite. He hadn't been able to
pull himself clear. It was very—gruesome. He was frozen
in. It nearly killed his mother. But you know, they are
noble people in their way. I believe that all she and Hugo
thought about, for the first week, was young Franz. How to
keep him from being overwhelmed by what had happened. In the midst of their grief, they always remembered to speak of it as if it had been Nicky's own fault, as if
he'd brought it on himself, through disobedience. But
Franz had his own ideas."

"What a tragedy. Why will people take risks?"

"Poor Franz. So when I think, as I often do, that he's not
the nicest man I've ever met, I always remind myself of
what's happened to him. Nor was having Hugo looking
over his shoulder all the time when he was growing up the
easiest thing in the world. Well, now you know about that,
Miss Glidden. And here comes Ev'rett."

Professor Pinckney came up and interrupted them. He
said good-by to Hazel while Coral went to do the same to
Jeanette, and then they drove off. He asked his wife what
she'd found to talk about for such a long time to Miss Glidden, and Coral replied that she'd been telling her some
Kerenyi family stories, to make her feel more at home.

"I told her about Nicky."

"Oh, Coral," he said, shaking his head.

"Well, it's just about the most interesting thing I know about them. And do you know what? Dorcas has never once mentioned it to her."

"That, no doubt," he said dryly, "was in order not to spoil your fun when, some day like today, you got your chance."

Hugo came to Franz again at last. "Now let's race," he said.

Franz shook his head.

"Come on. Come on. I challenge you. You can't refuse a challenge."

"I don't want to."

"Nonsense. Come on. We always raced. And you sometimes won, too. I'm older now. Still longer-legged, yes, but lots older."

"I don't want to."

"It would be good for you. A man who won't compete, Franz, had better begin to wonder about himself."

"I don't want to."

Hugo shrugged. "Well, then I'll go and make one last effort to get Miss Brittlesticks Glidden to skate with me." Off he went.

Ann, standing there, said, "Perhaps you should have. It might have reminded you what happens when you run from Father."

"I know what happens. But times have changed. A man of forty-three makes up the rules for a boy of fifteen. A man of sixty doesn't make them up for a man of thirty-two."

"That is true. But which pair of ages describes you and Father?"

"Both do. Or at least that is my prayer, Annie."

The sun was getting low, and most of the people, except those who, like the Kerenyis, had been prevented from an early start by a late dinner, were unlacing their boots and returning to their automobiles. Hugo came to Hazel and rose to his points with an impressive gouging of the ice.

"I hate for you to have stood alone here. Won't you try it? Please do. See how nicely Dorcas goes? This is your last chance. We will have to go soon. And there's almost nobody left to watch you."

It did not, in fact, fit Miss Glidden's ideas of herself to have so many people, including Dorcas, enjoying themselves at doing something she was afraid of. So she agreed. If Hugo would hold her up, she'd put on the skates. She would try. In a few moments she was ready, and he came up on the bank and found, when she tried to move, that she was very awkward, as might have been expected from her jerky, unathletic little movements during conversation, or when seated at table, so he almost carried her down to the edge of the ice. Dorcas had seen what was happening and came over to join in and encourage her friend.

It was certainly a bad idea, the whole thing. Hazel, hanging on to Hugo, touched the ice. He got her upright, held her that way so that she might propel herself gently forward on one foot, and eased just a little off from her. Instead of moving forward toward him, she lurched at him, and both of them lost ground. She dangled for a minute from his arm, and then went down onto the ice on her left side, pulling him almost to one knee with her.

She cried out.

Dorcas screamed. "Hugo," she said. "Be careful. Look what you've done."

He was already upright, and tugging at Miss Glidden. Dorcas's tone exasperated him, and he said, "Dorcas, I didn't let her fall on purpose. We hadn't even begun to move. Come on, Miss Glidden, get up now. Get up."

"She's just a beginner. Only a beginner. You ought to have held her fast."

"It's not my fault if she can't stand on her own two feet. Get up! I can't help you if you won't help yourself."

Hazel said, in a voice made even thinner by pain, "Get me back on that bank, Professor Kerenyi. I am injured."

When he had done so, she held her left wrist in her right hand and let the left hand dangle limply.

"Can you move your fingers? Are you sure it's not just mostly the fall?—you said you were so scared of them. If you can move the fingers, nothing's broken."

"I don't need you to tell me that." She sucked in her breath. Under the pink of the cold on her prim little face, she had turned a bad color. Probably she was hurt. "Help me to the automobile."

Bruce Cuttler came up with Ann and the children and asked what was the matter.

"Hazel Glidden had a little fall," said Hugo.

"Little!" said Aunt Dorcas furiously.

"Bruce, if you'll skate over there toward the bridge about five hundred feet, right near that landing there, you'll see a tall man with a blue-and-white stocking cap on. Get him. It's Doctor Skinner. I'm sure he won't mind having a look, even though it's Christmas." Hugo took off Hazel's skates, while Ann and Dorcas removed their own; then they took Miss Glidden, one on each side, to the car. Hugo went beside them, very awkward in his skating boots, going on the points. "Do you want to sit in front? Would you be more comfortable stretched out a little more on the back deck? I am sorry, you know." They put Hazel in front and Ann started the engine up and turned on the heater, and they waited for Bruce to come back with the doctor.

Bruce had meanwhile skated off in the direction Hugo had indicated but did not at first find his man. When he did, he went up to him, made sure he was Dr. Skinner, identified himself as the son-in-law of Hugo Kerenyi, and asked if they could speak for a moment.

Bruce said, "Ann, my wife, and I are worried about Mrs. Kerenyi, Doctor. I'm sure you understand why."

Dr. Skinner nodded, the pompon on his knitted stocking cap bobbing.

"We want you to be absolutely candid with us, even if you don't feel you should be with her or Hugo. She doesn't have—anything?"

Dr. Skinner pursed his lips and shook his head.

"We've felt the loss of vitality might explain the way she's been acting. You know what I mean?"

Dr. Skinner glanced at him and nodded.

"We were also wondering, if your answer was that she isn't sick, about the possibility of some sort of psychiatric care. Something intensive. I wouldn't know what exactly. A month at Menninger's or some shock, depending. Might that be indicated?"

Dr. Skinner shook his head.

Bruce said, rather coolly, "What the devil is wrong with the woman, Doctor?"

"Not much."

"What can you tell us that will help us?"

"Not much."

"You realize that the situation in that house is grave?"

"Why?"

"I don't think Hugo will go on like this."

"I can't say I'm surprised."

"He might elect to walk out."

"His choice, I'd say."

They both stood there with their backs to the cold wind, while Bruce considered what to say next, or, rather, how to put his next point. "Ann and I and the children are leaving early tomorrow morning to drop by Washington to see my own family before we go back to Chicago; but I'd be willing to delay our start and come to see you in your office to talk this over, if you'd feel more comfortable discussing it there. You understand."

Dr. Skinner shook his head. "No need."

"So you won't help us."

"Can't."

"Has everything reasonable been tried? All tests made? Consultations and all?"

Dr. Skinner nodded. "More than once."

"And it's your considered opinion that a psychiatrist won't be able to help?"

"Not without help from the patient."

"Could anyone?"

"A philosopher, maybe."

"I see we're wasting our time. One last question. Whose side do you take, Hugo's or Miriam's?"

"Science doesn't take sides."

Bruce smiled slightly. "Who ever thought doctors were scientists?" he said. "By the way, a woman who was with us, a friend of Mrs. Kerenyi's sister, just fell and hurt her wrist or arm or hand. Professor Kerenyi sent me to ask you if you'd mind coming to have a look at it. We're parked over there where you see the car lights on."

Dr. Skinner neither nodded nor shook his head, nor uttered a monosyllable, but skated away toward the parking area as fast as he could go. Hugo came to the edge of the ice to meet him and take him to the correct car, which both of them approached on their tiptoes. On the way the doctor asked how it had gone with Miriam, and Hugo said there'd been no change, that she hadn't come downstairs all day long. To which Dr. Skinner replied that he never had thought Hugo's plans for Christmas would work some miracle with her, and he'd never known of a last resort that worked in anything, medicine or anything else.

"I have the satisfaction of knowing I tried," said Hugo.

They went up to the car. "Now, who got the bumping?" the doctor asked.

"I fell," said Hazel.

"On her left side," said Dorcas.

"While Professor Kerenyi was teaching me to skate."

"She'd never been on skates before," said Dorcas.

"Which does not seem to me to fall into the category of helpful diagnostic information," Hugo said.

"Can you wiggle those fingers?" the doctor asked.

"Just what I told her," Hugo said.

"Ooooo."

The doctor manipulated gently.

"Ooooo."

"Wait a minute." Skinner went to his own car, which was not far away, got his kit, and came back with it. He taped the wrist and told her to get it X-rayed and to see her own doctor the next day, and wrote her a prescription for some pills to kill the pain. "You can get it rewritten by your own doctor, Miss Glidden, if you need to. It's not refillable."

"She's a registered pharmacist," said Dorcas.

"Then I don't need to warn you not to take too many." He gave her the name.

"As I expected."

Hugo accompanied Dr. Skinner over to the bank, where they both removed their boots. That done, it was time to go, but just at the end the doctor nudged Hugo.

"That's an inquisitive son-in-law you've got there," he said.

"Inquisitive about what?"

"Just about everything. Especially Miriam. I hope that wrist will be all right. Merry Christmas."

The family piled into the station wagon, doubling up, and went home, stopping at a drugstore on Nassau Street to fill Hazel's prescription, which Dorcas took in for her. Hazel asked how much it had been, and when Dorcas told her, said that it was full retail price.

"She's not used to that," Dorcas said. "Naturally."

"Naturally," Hugo agreed.

"Why did this have to happen to me so far away from home?" Hazel said.

"I feel it's all my fault," said Dorcas.

"Talk about it later," said Hugo.

Then they reached the house, and Hazel and Dorcas retired to Dorcas's room so that Hazel could rest, and one by one the others disappeared, too. But not before Hugo had announced that they should all come to the living room again, this time at seven o'clock, for their last evening together. Before he went up to change out of his heavy woolens himself, Hugo got the screen out of the closet back under the stairs and set it up in the living room, and set up his slide projector, too. It wouldn't have been a real Kerenyi family occasion if this Christmas had passed without his showing some of his slides. After he had changed clothes, he would have plenty of time, more than an hour, in which to select what the assembled family would see.

# four

# losing people

Six people attended the slide showing at seven, including Hugo. Old Mr. Kerenyi was tired from Christmas Eve and then the morning and the long dinner, and was remaining in his room until it was time for supper; the two Cuttler children were sent to play with their Christmas presents back in the library; Victoria was in her crib, asleep. The ingredients for hot buttered rum were out in the living room on a tray separate from the usual bar tray, which was also ready, and Hugo made it quickly, in pewter mugs, each one with a section of orange and lemon peel studded with cloves floating in it, and a piece of cinnamon bark. For himself and Ann he filled the mugs with hot cider, for Franz and Jeanette and Bruce and Dorcas with boiling water, in addition to the rum and butter. Hazel Glidden was dozing, so Dorcas had come downstairs by herself; she took the rum, but she was edgy and distant, not at all pleasant, really; in a mood. Miriam had not, of course, been heard from at all.

Hugo then turned out all the lights, except those on the Christmas tree and one huge standing lamp that looked as if it had been made for a men's club, with its scalloped parchment shade and polished wooden shaft as thick as a fence post. He had rolled it along on its broad wooden base to sit beside his chair behind the little table with the slide projector on it. He said, "Can everybody see the screen? We can look at anything out of the family past we want to, of course. I've got it all." He paused. "Any preferences? Just speak up." No one did, it being evident even to Bruce and Jeanette that Hugo had already decided everything. He then said, "I pulled out the box that has our trip up Old Rag in it, since it was mentioned last night, and I haven't looked at those slides for at least ten years myself. But first, I've arranged a little preamble."

He reached up and pulled the dangling chains of the fixtures of the lamp, but had to turn it back on and wait, because just then Franz (somewhat to Hugo's aggravation, for he didn't like interruptions when he was ready to show slides, as if it were works of art, his works of course, that he was showing), after sipping from his mug, said that he couldn't stomach the rum. He was sorry, but he'd have to get himself some whisky. When he had done so Hugo said, "When these lights go off this time, they stay off. Are you ready now for sure, Franz? Then here we go."

The first slide went on the screen. It showed, not in color but in black and white, a young woman with two children, their ages not too different from Ann and her children right now, possibly a bit younger. The slide was made, Hugo explained, from a snapshot, because it predated color transparencies, or anyway his color transparencies. "That is the beginning of it. Anything before is too anonymous, but there you can see intimations of what is to come, am I not right? Jeanette, do you recognize the little red-haired boy in short pants, about to have a temper tantrum, it would appear? And Bruce, you tell me who the broad-faced, brown-faced little girl might be, standing there so calmly, in a pleated skirt and a sailor collar. Have you guessed, both of you? Then we go on." The slide changed. The new scene had been taken at the seashore, and showed the same children, a year older, perhaps, in bathing suits, and standing between them, Hugo, younger and resplendent in striped swimming trunks, his hair cut very short. White sand glittered around their feet, and behind them was the line of the surf, and then the dark flat surface of the ocean until it met the sky. Franz was holding a fishing rod that looked three times too big for him, and Ann had a bucket. "You hated that fishing rod, do you remember, Franz?"

"I certainly did."

"But you learned how to cast into the surf with it all the same. You grew up into it. It is my theory, Jeanette, my contribution to the theory of child raising, that every child—or adult—should learn to do the kinds of recreation that are appropriate to wherever he is. If you're in the Alps, you climb, and so on. And that included, the summers we went to the shore, surf casting. Franz didn't like to, but he did it. He learned. Well, it is a truism, but no less true for the ism part, that nothing worthwhile can be entirely fun. Not even statistics, eh Franz?"

"I do not like even to see a fish to this day," Franz said.

Hugo laughed. "At least you have a specific reason for your dislike," he said. "That's better than inarticulate feelings or what they call 'not having a taste' for something, which doesn't mean anything at all, does it? Here's another scene at the seashore—we went just across from here, to Manasquan. We had the same cottage year after year—it belonged to some people named Stewart, I think it was, who raised setter dogs in Plainfield, and their cottage showed it. There it is behind us. Imagine all those shingles! Let's see. . . . That's Miriam holding Nicky, our second son, who died, as you know. That was the year he was born, so he's just about the age of your Victoria, Jeanette, but ill-fated." The slides went on and on. "Note how the costumes are modifying. Franz in knickers. And don't think, by the way, that the reason I'm in so many of them is simply my vanity. It is because Miriam hated to have her picture taken, and furthermore she was the most available person to push the button. So. The first color slides. The summer we went west on the train, about nineteen-fifty. The summer after your father died, Dorcas. That is a mountain sequoia, and the reason Miriam appears in front of it is that Aunt Dorcas was along to push the button in this case, and I was determined to have my entire family lined up before the General Grant tree." Hugo showed a dozen more of that trip—Los Angeles and San Francisco, Yellowstone, and Glacier Park. "And then this one, particularly for you, Bruce." It was the family posed in front of the Field Museum of Natural History in Chicago.

The slides went on, as did the years. Nicky disappeared, to everyone's relief. Hugo did not comment on it, but Franz did, pointing out that he had died that winter, nineteen-fifty-one, on the eleventh of February. "I just thought I'd remind you of the fact."

"Yes, of course, Franz," Hugo said. He went on through another fifteen slides at least, with Ann and Franz growing up before the eyes of Bruce and Jeanette. "And now, with that as an introduction, we come at last to Old Raggedy. Here we are in front of Monticello. All of us again. Some accommodating lady in colonial costume took this for us. I'd gone down to give a lecture in Charlottesville at the end of April, and Aunt Dorcas came down on the train on Friday with the children to join us as we drove north by way of Shenandoah Park and Washington, and that was when we stopped off, on Saturday, for our hike. Let's see. It was in nineteen-fifty-three, so Ann would have been about sixteen, and Franz seventeen. Am I right about that?"

Nobody said anything.

"Then here we go." One after another the slides came and went (accompanied by Hugo's commentary), beginning beside a parked car, with a backdrop of trees newly coming into leaf: Dorcas, the two children, and Hugo, with Miriam. "I used my timer for that. There wasn't anybody around to help."

"Look at Mother," Franz said.

"It is interesting, isn't it?"

Dorcas said, "It was more that day than turning her face away from the camera. She wouldn't march with the rest of us. I felt I had to, Hugo, but she wouldn't." Dorcas's voice went up. "It wasn't fair." She seemed to be getting very agitated, moving in her chair, her fingers never still.

"I'd forgotten."

"Well, I haven't."

Another slide: the little family setting off up a path, through an aisle of trees all the clear colors of early spring, with a sprinkling of redbuds in bloom. "You had on shorts, too, Annie. There must not have been mosquitoes yet." Another slide, more or less the same. Then one of Franz, glowering, as he so often seemed to, at the camera, holding a walking staff. "There's you and the stick we cut for you, looking like Saint Christopher." Another slide: Franz, taken from an angle, to show the rucksack he was carrying. "Part of our lunch. You really were small for your age—that was a postage stamp of a rucksack, but it looks enormous on your back." More slides: the family amidst great jumbled boulders as they ascended the mountain's flank, and out on ledges, with backdrops of other mountains rolling away toward the north and south; cliffs; Hugo carrying another rucksack, of leather like his shorts, that on him looked undersized. There was one of Miriam alone, taken through an odd configuration of rocks, a kind of tunnel, when she wasn't looking. There was a fine one of Dorcas standing amidst a scattering of trillium, and others, taken close up, of trillium and of all the other spring flowers for which, Hugo explained, the walk was noted. "It's almost over. Here we are, all of us, soaking our feet in the Hughes River—certainly an impressive name for that brook. And here is the last of them. Here we are, back by the car, sunburned and dirty, but content. That was a day!" Hugo exclaimed.

He pulled on one light. "What a wonderful invention the camera is, after all. What else is civilization but reverence for the study of the fine and the noble out of human experience, and the camera has added a new dimension: every man may have his life illustrated. Who wants another hot buttered rum?"

He hurried to the kitchen to reheat the water and cider, returned and made the drinks, glanced at his wrist watch, said there was still time (for dinner had been over so late and the children were still quiet) for more slides.

Suddenly Aunt Dorcas got to her feet. She walked nervously to the piano and put her mug back on its proper tray, then returned to the group of chairs, but she did not sit down again. "I think I will go," she said. "I think it is best if I get Hazel and go now. I don't like seeing the slides."

Hugo looked first at her, then at Ann. "Oh-oh. I recognize that tone from days of yore, Aunt Dorcas. Could it be that one of your famous scenes is about to begin? Well, even they are a part of the Kerenyi tradition."

"You enjoyed yourself." There was an unexpected—and for these scenes, uncharacteristic—little quaver in Dorcas's voice. "You always enjoyed yourself. I only remember being ordered around."

"Come now, Dorcas."

"Like a soldier on a forced march."

"Well, nobody denies, least of all me, that I have my authoritarian side. But I was always a benevolent despot. Come now, Dorcas, let *us* not argue."

"I was the good soldier, and my sister got out of more and more things. I filled in, but I didn't like it."

"Is that true, Aunt Dorcas?" said Franz. "About Mother?"

"Absolutely. That day in Virginia, and all the others, too."

Hugo said, "She did find ways in which to do as she pleased."

"To avoid being a slave," Dorcas said.

"You push your point to absurdity, Dorcas. Our family

has always, until recently, remained within the generally accepted definition of the normal. I rest my case on that."

"A slave is a human being who has to do what he is told to do. It is not a New England conception of human relationships."

"I thought that in New England one had relations but not relationships." Hugo laughed. "But let's continue our slide tour. Let's go on to Franz's wedding. And then—"

"The worst of it all, in Virginia, was at the end, when you made me drink from your dirty canteen, Hugo, the mouth of your canteen that all of you had been using for hours, rather than take a drink from that lovely stream. And why? Not because it was bad, the water . . ."

"It might have been."

"You didn't know. Not because it was bad, but because your orders for the day were not to use natural water, because natural water may sometimes have germs; therefore good soldiers carry canteens and drink from them and don't take any chances. Don't drink the water which might have germs, drink from a canteen which certainly has them. It was disgusting. The whole thing was disgusting."

Dorcas moved so that her back was square to the screen. "I won't see any more slides. I *won't*. I will take Hazel home right now, as soon as I can get ready to go. I *will*."

Hugo at once became conciliatory. "Come now, Aunt Dorcas. You can't do that. Stay for supper. I promise I will speak only softly. Don't go away." He got up and reached for her hand, but she snatched it back. "We have come, in this family, to a stage of divisions and separations at best, and I do not want them to be increased, nor should you. You are our only aunt or uncle. You must stay."

"You are right about the divisions and separations," Dorcas said, unrelenting. "And you should know, Hugo, that they are your own doing. And so should all of you," she added, addressing the next generation. "I don't mind saying this in front of all of you. It's what I think, and you should hear it. They are your doing, Hugo. Your insistence on talking loudest, talking longest, having things the way you want them, getting your own way, is what has caused them. But I want to tell you this, too: you've needed co-operation. You haven't been getting your own way, people have given it to you. Without the co-operation of other people, you can't have it at all. Your—I'll call it what I think it is—your tyranny has existed only because there was consent to it. Now you have come to the end of that consent, and when you talk about changing things and rejuvenation, all it means is that you know it's at an end and so you've got to go out and find new people to push and shove, because who they are hasn't ever mattered nearly so much to you as that there should be some. All of what you do—it only works as long as a person agrees to stay and let it. I'm not excusing Miriam for what she seems to be doing. She chose you, and she ought to stick by that, and ought to have fought you and not given in so much. But I also want to say that she's finally discovered, and maybe it was on Old Raggedy that she first discovered it, that all she has to do is to walk off, and you're helpless. I'm discovering the same thing—did some time back. What's more, you've given all of us a lesson today in how your orders work, how they hurt the innocent, and how when they then lie helpless in front of you, you kick at them. Never again. You won't ever get the chance to make me, or any friend of mine, do what you want us to do again, Hugo."

She walked over to him, so that they were directly confronting each other. "I don't like you and I never have. I hope that I never, under any circumstances, for any reason, or by any accident, see you again in all my life. And I forbid you to come to my funeral if I die first."

Suddenly her mouth turned down at the corners; she burst into tears and hurried out of the room.

"Well," Hugo said. "Well. That's rather a bigger scene than usual." He looked around at his embarrassed family, but didn't give anyone a chance to say anything. "I hardly feel it necessary to comment on what she said, the motives are so transparent and pathetic—the spinster sister, resenting not kindnesses but the fact that they are necessary. And then, what it comes down to is that she doesn't like me because I am a man, with a man's energies and will." He shrugged. "I've always heard that relationships such as the one she has contracted—well, that they intensify the sexual antagonisms such people feel—misandry, you know—and that, moreover, offering but partial pleasures, they are profoundly unsettling. We all understand what I mean."

Ann said, "We can't let her go like that. I'll see if they won't come down and have sandwiches with us before they leave."

Hugo said, "Yes, do. And you may tell her I do not demand an apology."

When Ann got upstairs to Dorcas's room, Hazel was in the bathroom and Dorcas was packing her bag. Ann kept her from putting her nightgown in it. "Aunt Dorcas, don't leave like this. It's been such a hard time. Don't end it like this."

Dorcas said, "What else can I do with dignity? I have finally quarreled, deeply and seriously, with your father."

"He asked me to tell you he wasn't offended. We want you and Hazel to stay and have turkey sandwiches with us."

"I couldn't stay in the same room with him, much less sit down at table with him. I will never eat another meal in this house."

"Are you serious?"

"Absolutely."

"I don't think he quite deserves what you've said to him."

"I do."

"But not now, anyway."

"Above all now."

"You always get angry with Father. We all joke about it."

"This isn't like that." Dorcas smiled. She laid the nightgown down and, as yieldingly as she was able, kissed her niece's cheek. "There. I wanted to do that, too. Annie, I don't love you any less. Or Franz either, as far as that goes. I won't forget you, and I hope you won't forget me."

"You mean that we can come to your funeral?"

"I know that was a quirky thing to say. But it just occurred to me. Maybe it was the talk last night about graves. I just couldn't bear to think that I'd got that man out of my life at last, and that he might triumph over me in the end."

Ann gave up. "Then what about the turkey and mincemeat pie that Mrs. Vendredy put aside for you? You'll take them with you?"

"That would be nice. I won't see your father, but I won't waste his food. Put it on the table right by the front door. I don't intend even to look in the living room as I go by. Put it where I'll see it. Put it where I won't have to ask you where it is. I'll have to speak to Miriam now. I want her to hear about this from me first."

Ann didn't want to leave. "I'm so sorry, Dorcas," she said, lingering by the door.

"Don't be. It's been cooking up for a long time. I didn't intend to come back for another of these family things again. I shouldn't have given in to your father. It was a mistake. I gave in, and there's been trouble from it. Hazel let him talk her out onto the ice, and there was trouble from that. He can't be whole himself without carving into the room that belongs to other people, Ann, just remember that."

"What bothers me more, Dorcas, is that I'm beginning to sense what all this is going to cost before we're through."

Dorcas nodded. "Annie, have you kept the Loeb Classics I gave you when you still read your ancient languages? Or have you thrown them away?"

"Of course I haven't thrown them away. What an idea! I have them all together in a box."

"I'm so relieved. I'm going to send you another—I've kept a list somewhere of what you have. Don't worry, I don't expect you to read it now. Just put it in the box with the others. For later on. And I'm going to leave you mine— the ones you don't have. There. I've promised them to you."

"So Father's not even allowed to come to your funeral, but I get a legacy."

"This is precisely correct. What I'm going to say now lots of people would consider old-fashioned, but I believe it. You'll go back to them, Ann, because when everything else goes hollow, the Classics endure."

While Hazel sat on the bed, touching the bandage and the skin around the bandage of her injured wrist, Dorcas went in to Miriam, whom she found, as she had that morning, on her chaise longue. Miriam looked pale and sad, although that might have been the dim light. She was wearing the new wool stole that the Cuttlers had brought to her, and she was reading.

Dorcas said, "There isn't enough light in here to read by."

And Miriam: "How upset you look."

"Sister, I have come to say good-by. I have quarreled with Hugo. Badly. There's no reason to go into how or why."

"Really quarreled? Or just bickering?"

"There's something different about this time. I have insulted him." She told Miriam about Hazel's accident. "But," she said, "I have quarreled with Hugo not only for things he has done, but for what he is. I've told him what he is, in front of everybody. I suppose we could both pretend to overlook it, but I do not want to. I will not be back."

Miriam made a gesture, perhaps signifying merely that she had heard.

"You have backed out, and I see no reason for me to keep up the connection, as, off and on, I've tried to do over the years."

"Not just you, Dorcas."

"No, of course not. No more. I will never again make the trip from King of Prussia to Budapest."

Miriam said, "And what about Northampton? The road we traveled so companionably on together last night?"

"I don't like fanciful language, as you know. But I'll go along with it just for now. You have cost both of us the road to Northampton that we could travel together, Miriam. That is the cost of what you have done. That is the cost of it. Whatever happens here, I do not want to go on that road with you again. And I don't believe that you're doing what you think you're doing, either." Dorcas came nearer the chaise longue, and stood unbending, straight-backed. "I happen to think that what you're doing is trapping yourself. You've trapped yourself by this cowardly backing out. You've trapped yourself, not where you may think you are, not at all. You've trapped yourself in Budapest forever."

Miriam was puzzled. "But—how?"

"This time you've really given in to him," Dorcas replied. "That's what it comes down to. He's finally beaten you. He's bellowed and rammed at you until you're sneaking off to hide."

To which Miriam did not reply.

"That's why I won't be back. We'll write—until perhaps the day comes, I don't say it won't, when it will feel all right to see you again."

Miriam said, "One thing I have to say to you. I believe, when you come to think about it, that you will realize that your King of Prussia is as far from Northampton as what you wish to call my Budapest. And all roads are blocked."

Dorcas backed away. "Say no more," she whispered.

"So then that is what we've accomplished, you and I, this Christmas," Miriam added. "A mere obstruction of the traffic."

Aunt Dorcas made a stiff little bow and left the room.

There was, however, still a question she had wanted to pose to Miriam but had not had the courage for. She changed her mind about it, though, and left Hazel one final time to go and knock on Miriam's door, so softly it couldn't be heard down in the living room. There was no answer. Miriam's sitting room was dark, and there was faint light from under the bedroom door. It didn't matter. Dorcas didn't ask the question; instead, she wrote it down on a piece of paper she found on Miriam's writing desk, turned on a light and wrote it:

Miriam: You asked me last night if I'd ever really wanted to come to spend my holidays and vacations with you. I tried to answer, and it sounded ungrateful. I don't think we should leave it that way. I don't think your question is fair unless I get to ask one too. The question I'd ask back is this: Sister, did you ever really want me?                                            D.

She left the note on the desk. Sooner or later Miriam would find it there.

Aunt Dorcas's departure, which she carried out exactly as she said she would, taking Hazel Glidden through the hall without even looking into the living room, rather dampened the interest in slides. Hugo showed a few of the Kerenyi-Cotton wedding, but then stopped. It was time for supper anyway, eight o'clock, so he got his father and everyone pitched in and prepared it.

The tradition of the Kerenyi house, where supper in the evening following a midday turkey dinner was concerned, was sandwiches made with freshly grated horse-radish mixed with mayonnaise spread on them, and Ann and

Jeanette made them that way for everybody except the Cuttler children, who didn't like hot condiments. Hugo opened beer, and a bottle of Beaujolais, too, as well as one of the Loibner wine of the night before for his father, and they sat around the big, oilcloth-covered kitchen table and ate. When that was over, Mr. Kerenyi said that he was tired and would go on out home, and they all went to the front hall to see him off. Hugo asked him if he wanted to see Miriam again, or to try to, but Mr. Kerenyi said no, he would not do so this evening. He contrived a moment, in the confusion of getting coats, looking for car keys, and shoving stray ice skates back into a closet, to talk to Ann.

"What do you say, Annie?" he asked. "What will happen now?"

"I'm afraid of the worst. I'll try with Father, but . . ." Her eyes filled with tears, for the first time. "Mother is a lost cause, for now."

"Maybe for always. I've been thinking about her, and I've put what is wrong into words, Annie. It is simple. She has lost her hold on life. That is the trouble. No matter how subtle are the reasons that she gives, or how intentional what she says has happened, that is it. She has lost her hold on life. It has run out—a cup that was never full to begin with, to use Hugo's phrase. As in most important things, Annie, there is first the condition, made out of the whole fiber of the person, and then the description and rationalization of it. But that is what it is. It is a failure of energy."

Everyone said good-by to him then, Ann, and young Franz, too, with great feeling, for it might well be the last time.

Hugo drove silently and slowly past the university buildings and on out through the west end of town toward Hopewell and Bucks County, through some of the open countryside that still survived around a Princeton now beleaguered by real-estate development. After perhaps twenty minutes of such unaccustomed carefulness, he turned off the highway into a long drive edged with sycamore trees whose mottled trunks shone in the headlights of the car as it swung through the big curve toward the house and its dependent buildings, the home for the affluent elderly in which Mr. Kerenyi lived. Hugo stopped at the steps, which led up to a wide, deep terrace and to the front door.

Mr. Kerenyi said, "You seem to be a man with something on his mind. Perhaps you had better tell me."

"Perhaps I had. I haven't been sure, but yes, I think I ought to. It has seemed inconsiderate, because what I have to say isn't, I suppose, very definite, but—well, let me ask you: how did you think it went?"

"About as I expected."

"And how was that?"

The old man sighed, locked and then disengaged his gloved fingers several times, and at length replied, "Let me answer to one side of your question. I will make a confession. I am ashamed, in a way, to admit it, but it is like some of the things we octogenarians must admit to our doctors. We find them shameful, but we must get used to admitting them. My confession is this: I cannot help but think first of my own comfort. I think of your household as it affects me. It is not there because of me, of course, it is not my doing, but in part it is the way it is because of me, and that has not been done unselfishly. I have not made it, but I have made it the way I want it, insofar as I can. And you have been willing—naturally an essential precondition. Like you, then, I like my own way. Even more, I like my own ways now. Do I now face some painful dislocation? I am asking myself that—and the stars and the gods. Do I? Some event I hadn't foreseen that might make it impossible for me to continue to the end as I have it all planned and arranged? I worry about that. Not about much more. It is humiliating."

"The danger is real."

"I am aware of that. I haven't yet taken to worrying about things that don't exist at all. No doubt it will come— perhaps even as a relief."

"I feel I've tried as much as anyone could expect of me. Including, finally, this holiday, which has not gone as I expected it to. It has been worse."

"There is nothing I can say, particularly as I can't imagine how you expected it to go."

"And what is more, I'm not going on this way. I meant that when I said it. That is what I have on my mind tonight. That is what I have to say to you. My old life is at an end."

"It will be boring for your friends."

Hugo smiled. "Not at first."

"How will she manage?"

"How will I?"

"But how will she?"

"I don't know."

"And neither, of course, is my worry. Well, I remind you of one thing: nothing ever grows without seeds having been planted. Had you asked my advice about this Christmas, about your whole plan for it, bringing everyone together and all, I might have warned you that you were risking more than you stood to gain. You were running the danger of learning more than you would want to. For example, this: that for your plan to work you would have had to return to the past and do things differently as far back as you could remember."

"Hard advice to follow, Father."

"Not hard, Hugo. Impossible."

"And what is more, one must give the past its place, but the future must have its place, too."

The old man opened his door, and Hugo got out to make sure he climbed the steps safely. They rang for the attendant, who was soon there, a little sleepy and sullen, working overtime on the holiday; but when he saw Mr. Kerenyi he smiled, for the old man's tips had been among the largest.

When Hugo got back to his own house he found that Bruce and Jeanette had both gone to bed, because everyone would be traveling again tomorrow, and the children were in bed too, of course. But Ann and Franz had waited up for him. There had to be a talk among the three of them, added to all the others of the day. They went back into Hugo's little study, Franz and Hugo each with a drink, Ann without one, and sat down in the worn overstuffed furniture.

Hugo said, "I suppose we must have a summing up."

Ann said, "How can we sum it up?"

"We are all losing Miriam. I think we all have to agree on that. Doesn't that do it?"

Ann replied, "Not quite. We must remind ourselves that Mother is losing, too."

Hugo said, with a kind of coldness in his voice, "Yes, you are right. She is losing everything. I will win after all, because I am choosing that which goes on, more life, and all that is comprised therein."

Ann said, "Must we put it in terms of losing and winning?"

Hugo frowned. "I'm tired of blaming Miriam, and of reproaching her. It is boring—of me and for me. So I won't start to do it again now, and won't comment."

"And anyway, we won't, Franz and I, I suppose, lose her necessarily in quite the sense you may. If I'm following the drift of your meaning. I wonder if I am."

"Oh, it's clear enough." Everyone thought about that clarity. "The house should be sold," Hugo said, "in any case."

"That hurts," said Ann.

"Yes. It is the place where we have been a family," Hugo said. "That was on my mind when I planned this reunion, that idea. I thought you should both see it again, fully populated. To reinforce memories, eh, Franz?"

Franz did not look at him.

"So you had already thought ahead that far," was Ann's comment.

"I fervently hoped it would turn out to be unnecessary foresight."

"Do contingency plans go with fervent hope, I wonder?"

"Annie, I had little enough reason to be hopeful. Look—" He got from a cabinet above his desk several leather notebooks. "These are the notes I keep, or sometimes the rough drafts, year by year, of what will one day be our family history. When I retire, I will put it all together, for you and Franz and your children. I have been going back through it, looking for Miriam. Do you know what I mean? Looking for the first traces, the first glimpses of the ugly little snout of what I must call the monstrous beast that now dens in this house. I have found them, I think, and they are distant, back many years in some cases. I could have shown you those, in the slides tonight, for Old Rag was certainly not the first and not the worst case. There was the time I rescued her—that is how my entry reads in these notebooks—rescued her from the house of death where her father lay dying month after month, with Dorcas changing his bed for him and beseeching his approval, reading to him, breathing out Latin verse into the air that stank of the flesh's corruption, yes, that so frighteningly gentle grandfather of yours, never, as I do, saying I want this and this and this, yet wanting and taking all his daughters could give and more. That horrible farmhouse belonging to your great-aunt or third cousin or whatever she was, who lay in her own bedroom slobbering to herself the hymns of the vegetable people. I tell you, I figuratively opened windows in that house to let the wind blow through until my arms ached, and finally I had to take Miriam away, almost by force. It *was* a rescue; she owed me a great deal for it. Without me . . . who knows? But that capacity, if you want to call it that, to subside into being a kind of dumb handmaiden to Father Baxter—isn't that a first glimpse? Wasn't it one when she walked along the beach, sometimes almost all night long, in those days when Franz was learning to cast into the surf? Most people like to walk along the beach, but for some the ocean is a great danger. She is one of those. And the way she curled up, like a threatened caterpillar, when Nicky died, wouldn't uncurl, month after month, year, it seemed, after year. What about that? People used to lose half their children. Mortality is a fact of life. It was not healthy, no. Well, I could go on. . . ."

"Don't. I can think about it for myself. I'd rather have my own version," Ann said.

"You will read mine when it is ready. And it will be accurate and documented, even with photographs. History cannot change anything, but it can help us to understand. It is for that reason that I will write it all down."

Some time passed while Hugo put his notebooks away. Then Ann said, "I want to ask a great, really a great favor of you."

Hugo stopped, holding the last of the notebooks in his hands. "Of course," he said warily.

"Wait. Can't you wait? Can't it be given more time? Wait a year. Give the situation another year and see if she doesn't pull out of it."

"I do not want to."

"But you should want to. Just a year, for my sake."

"I don't have a year to waste."

"You assume it will be wasted. Perhaps it won't be."

Hugo began to get irritated. "No. Now let us stop this."

"Father, it is only reasonable to give her more time."

Hugo raised his voice. "I have given her enough. I said today what I think. Let it be as it is. Let her be as she wants to be. I am going on without her."

Ann said firmly, "Eagerly, it seems to me. A little too eagerly."

And now Hugo did get angry. "This is not a matter

which we should discuss any more. It is between your mother and me, and it is my own life and I will lead it as I want to. You must mind your own business."

"Christ!" Franz muttered. He got another drink.

Ann answered back, "Of course it is my business. And don't bully me, Father. It can't be done any more. I intend to say what I please about this subject. You can't shut me up just because you don't want to have to hear what I want to say."

Surprisingly, Hugo subsided. "No, I mustn't bully you. I mustn't argue with you. No, I agree. It is a measure of my changed situation that I did not argue with Bruce tonight, either. I wanted to. I planned to when I got the chance, but I didn't do it. We can't have more arguments, can we?"

"Over what?" Ann asked, curious.

"He quizzed Doctor Skinner. It was not his place to ask him questions. A year ago I would not have tolerated it, but now I must." Hugo pointed. "Because of you. Because I must not lose you, too."

"You aren't likely to. Well, I can't force you to do as I ask, to wait, but remember that I asked it. Think about it."

"There's no use." Hugo put the last notebook away.

Then Ann asked, "What will you do next, Father?"

"Who knows? More dinners with the Pinckneys. I'll go to Germany this summer, as I've planned, only as a bachelor, or a man separated from his wife, or a man getting a divorce. And so on. Yes, *and so on!* You heard me this afternoon. I meant what I said." He hesitated. "I am from a generation that doesn't find it easy to talk about such things to its children, but let me just say that I am still possessed of all my powers. I hope that is both delicate and comprehensible. Most people would say that that is another score I have to settle with Miriam—but no. You're right, that's not the way to put it. A failure of hers for which I must find compensations. Alternatives. I like that better. That is what I will do."

"So your late style will consist of that," said Ann.

"I will go where it takes me," said Hugo. "And I will not look back."

"You do have a heartless streak in you."

He said, "Will you finally take her side, Sphinx?"

Ann shook her head.

Hugo said more brightly, "Well, there is one thing, I believe, that all this trouble has done, and I'm very thankful for it. It has, if in a thorny, difficult way, brought me to feel closer once again to both of you. I feel that I have opened up the possibility, that we all have, of becoming friends once more, I with my children, you with your father. Only now we are all adults together. I have lost my wife, but I have regained my children, as friends. You have grown older and therefore have come to meet me, and I—I am turning to welcome you, and we shall find each other in middle ground, new ground, perhaps happier ground. That is something positive that has happened."

"Yes, if it does happen, that will be positive," Ann said.

"One can move around so easily now. I will be lonely, I suppose. I will depend on you. I will learn how to depend on both of you. We must see each other. I can take places in the summer, perhaps, where you can come to visit me, both of you, with your families. I will like that. That is why I didn't quarrel with Bruce."

"I'm glad you didn't."

Hugo said, "You are very silent, Franz. What have you to say?"

Franz drank his drink straight down, while they watched, then got up and went for a final time, he said, to the piano out in the other room and the bar set up on top of it. He was unsteady on his feet; it couldn't be avoided, the knowledge of that. Hugo watched him when he returned, too (Ann did not; she looked away), saw him slump back into his chair and land on one side so that he bumped the arm, slid down sideways, and spilled some of his new drink on his trousers.

"We all know you can swallow, but what have you to say?" Hugo asked again.

"All right, all right, Father. You want me to talk, so I will. I'll say that I'm scared to death. It's taken me you can't imagine how much worry and work and lost time and sleepless nights and all the whole goddamn rest of it to get myself to where I feel like a reasonably whole man—oh, not all the time, but sometimes, at least, like sometimes when I'm getting at some new information, or—my generation finds saying things like this so goddamn easy, you know—or when I'm mounting my wife, to take another example."

"Franz!"

"Yes, that's what I mean. It's like that, Father."

Ann tried to interrupt. "Let's not talk any more tonight. We're all too tense. Let's go to bed."

"No. I'm going on."

"Please, Franz. Not tonight."

"Shut up, Annie. You begged me to try to influence Father. Well, I'm going to—in my own way." He turned back to Hugo. "I feel like a man, then, at those times, independent of you and independent, in a different way, of Mother, and of the way I feel about both of you, and the ways you've taught me to feel. Independent of a whole lot of things: little memories and big memories, like all the times I heard you say, 'Do this, Franz,' or 'Don't do that, Franz,' or like leaving that little bastard brother to drown all by himself. But now I'm scared again. I feel like I'm slipping back down a mountainside. Just being in this house makes me feel that way, which is something I've never known before, but then I've been developing a special method for seeing things clearly." He held up his glass. "This house does it, yes, and the water where Nick took his count of three—and thanks for taking us all near there today, I really appreciated it; it showed how delicate you are in your feelings—"

Hugo interrupted. "That was eighteen years ago, and

nobody ever blamed you for it. You should have put it out of your mind long since. Not to do so is unmanly, Franz."

"Unmanly!" Franz snorted his laugh. "Well, where was I? Slipping down a mountainside. That's it. I'm slipping back down a mountainside I've only just managed to climb, that's what I feel like. I'm being pushed from above and pulled from behind, and I'm slipping back down. I ask myself, could I be the prisoner who only gets as far as the gate every time he tries to escape? But no. That's not how I feel *when I'm away from you.* I do escape. Do you understand? Then, I feel myself a man. Et cetera, et cetera, as you put it. Do you find my figures of speech banal? Well, so is my condition. Falling down mountains, locked in jail: those tell what I feel like, or did, do right now, don't always any more, so forgive my lack of elegance in diction and freshness of style. I'm not a writer like you; I'm a statistician, don't forget. Getting us here for Christmas, to return to the main thread of my argument, that's not meeting us, grownup to grownup. That's reducing us. Trying to cut us back down to child-size bites for your big sharp teeth. And then twisting us all up in this mess you've got yourselves into, both of you. I don't want it. I don't want anything to do with it. I don't want to be a little boy in this house, having to worry about what I do, whether it's right or wrong. Get out of this house; I don't give a damn. I don't give a damn what happens to either of you. I can't afford to. And as far as you and I becoming friends is concerned, I don't want any part of that, either. No, you're not going to get away with that. Let me tell you, having had you for a father is enough of you for any one man's lifetime."

"Stop it, Franzie, stop it!" Ann cried out. "You're drunk, and you don't mean half of it and you'll be sorry."

"I am drunk, and I may be sorry. But what I've said is the truth. As to whether a person can mean it when he says the truth—that's one of your profound questions, and not

the neat, limited kind I like to ask myself. Me, I'll take statistics. They don't lead you anywhere too nasty."

Hugo sat and looked at him, thoughtfully. Finally he
said, "Well, I did ask you to speak, but I certainly did not
want you to say what you've just said. I would not have
asked to hear that, just now. I do not consider it dignified
or necessary to reply."

Franz said sarcastically, "No, don't. Aunt Dorcas and I,
we belong in the same low category. Consider our motives
and don't bother yourself any further."

Hugo looked at his watch. He got up. "I think I will go
to meet Monique's bus," he said.

"Father," Ann said, "forgive Franz."

"Let him forgive himself."

Hugo went out into the hall, and then outside.

Ann said, "That was a terrible thing to do, Franz."

"He'll reinterpret it. You know him. He deserves to hear
it, once in his life. And what is more, I deserved the
chance to say it. And I'll remember it the way it was
meant."

"Yes, I think you will. That is the saddest part of all."

"It's a funny thing, Ann," he said. "I've learned just one
thing from this holiday. Only one, really. But it's their full
revenge for what I've said to both of them. I've learned I
never mattered so very much. I've learned that I was a cas-
ualty on the edge, in a skirmish. Or so I think. I don't know
whether I can face that. Not really. How can I and continue to think that what became of me counts enough to
bear it, after all?"

"I don't think I understand."

"Try what I'm using and you will. Maybe." Franz
walked back to the living room and made himself a night-
cap of ice cubes and whisky.

He said good night to his sister and climbed the stairs to
his room. Jeanette was awake and waiting for him, but he
did not talk with her, other than to say that she'd get her

way: they'd probably never see Hugo or Miriam again. Then he got into bed and sat, with the bedside light on, propped up on his pillow, finishing his dark drink. That was how he fell asleep, and the glass tipped over in his hand, the last of it running down onto his bare arm. Even the ice cubes, melting against his skin, did not awaken him.

On her way to bed Ann stopped by her mother's sitting room and found, as Dorcas had before her, that it was dark and empty, but that there was a light on in the bedroom. She knocked, and after a considerable delay, as if a reply required some kind of decision, Miriam called to her to come in. She was in bed, with a litter of open books around her, eight or ten, lying, some face up, some face down, on bed, bedside table, and floor; but she was not reading and did not seem to have been.

She said, "I've retreated still farther. I'm counting up costs and I'm thinking, Annie."

"What about?"

"About how it will be in this house after everyone has gone tomorrow. For me."

"Finally empty," Ann said, with deliberate ambiguity.

"Yes. I've been estimating how empty."

"Will you come down to see us off?"

"Possibly. There's no harm in that."

"It will be uncomfortable."

"Oh, that—"

"I don't mean what you think. Franz quarreled painfully with Father."

"I'm not surprised. Well, Hugo long ago decided Franz was unworthy of him. This will confirm it."

Ann shuddered. "Mother, you realize that Father is surely going to . . . dissolve all this. Including this nest of books. I mean house and all."

"It doesn't matter."

"What will you do?"

"Be glad, I hope."

"Grandfather thinks you've lost your hold on life, as he puts it. Is that so?"

"I don't know."

"Father has gone to meet Monique's bus."

"It's a cold night."

"It certainly is," Ann said.

"Has Franzie gone to bed?"

"Yes. Just ahead of me. Drunk."

"Someday, Annie, will you tell him something? Will you tell him that of all of you who tried today to change my intentions, he came the closest to success. He, you see, did not talk about going on, about the future. He tried to arouse the wish to go back, to do something over, to do something better that had been badly done before, to change not what is or will be but what was. The hunger to do that, it seems, is the last to fade. Will you tell him someday?" Miriam asked.

"I'll tell him," Ann replied.

She kissed her mother and said good night, and climbed the stairs to her own bedroom. Bruce was already sound asleep, but she did not sleep, not for a long time. She lay awake for what seemed like hour after hour, thinking of what had happened, and of what it might mean to her; and there was a bleakness to her thoughts that was not usual for her, and that, reflecting upon it, she could not quite account for. She was glad for Bruce beside her, his black hair and shadow of beard very dark against the white pillow slip; for he was so certain of what was convenient and possible, and that would be her protection as the sorry story of her mother and father unfolded and concluded. That was what he was there for. Always had been, since first she had "discovered" him, living on the third floor, caught him looking at her. And yet . . . A remark of Miriam's came back to her which had been cast in her mother's favored sibylline mode: that Miriam was showing her a way. It nagged at her—raised the question of what unknown inheritance, unknown and perhaps unwanted, these two days had revealed, waiting for her. Well, it was only *a* way, one of many. And in between, there were children to be brought up.

The eleven o'clock bus was late, and Hugo waited nearly half an hour, sitting down the block from the stop nearest the Kerenyi house, his engine idling, the heater on. Several passengers got off, but only one of them started down the dark side street in the right direction. After looking, or not quite looking, wondering, perhaps, if there was anyone to see him, he turned the corner and pulled up beside her, for it was Monique. He wound down the window on the passenger side and leaned over to call out softly, "Merry Christmas again." She got in and remarked that he hadn't waited where he usually did and she'd thought he hadn't come for her.

"It occurred to me that perhaps I shouldn't wait right by the stop for you. Sooner or later somebody who knows one of us will notice." He was jocular. "I must think of your reputation."

At the corner where he should have turned into his own street, he asked instead, "Do you mind if we drive around just for a few minutes before we go home?"

She shook her head. It was warm in the car and she unbuttoned her tight coat collar, revealing a little of the scarf Miriam had given her; but of course Hugo had never seen it, and didn't know it was from his son.

"All in all, it's gone very badly."

"I'm so sorry."

"It can't be helped. It has grown intolerable. It has taken a family Christmas to make me face it squarely. The only thing that has made it tolerable for me this year, I think, as I look back over it, is you."

She didn't reply.

He told her some of the things that had happened. He described, amusingly, the "trivial little accident" of Miss

Glidden's fall, putting in details to point up its absurdity, such as Aunt Dorcas's remark that Miss Glidden was afraid of dropping things. "Who wouldn't be, if a thousand pills would be rolling around on the floor when you did. Of course it won't be funny if she's really hurt, but she isn't, I'm sure. I know Skinny. He didn't think so either." Hugo came to a stop, down by another part of Carnegie Lake. He had a faint, faint and faintly agreeable, sense of the vulgarity of what he was going to do, as he had it worked out in his mind, and a not so agreeable sense of its possible absurdity; but he did not really care. A man who wants new experience must look for it, and must, as it could be put, expose himself, if necessary, to . . . reversals.

He said, "I've quarreled seriously with Franz, too. He has certainly not grown up to be the man I would have liked him to be. No doubt it's partly my fault, but I only tried to chisel the outside; I can't be held responsible for flaws in the stone. Yes, many things have gone wrong, but don't worry, I intend to go on."

"Oh, yes. You must. And you will."

"Yes, I will."

It took, at that final second, more courage than he'd thought it would, to ask her the next question.

"Monique, may I kiss you?"

She shook her head.

"You shake your head so gently, as if your mind were not quite made up—for I do you too much credit to suppose you could be coquettish. May I not, Monique? Please, may I not kiss you?" He captured her left hand.

She shook her head again, perhaps just a little bit harder.

"No?"

"No," she said.

"It would mean so much to me."

"I'm sorry."

He was not quite sure how to proceed. They sat a few

moments. Then he asked, "Would you let me if I were not married?"

"I don't know."

"Would you let me if I were thirty years younger?"

"Yes."

He had not expected that answer. "Do you mean that?" he asked sharply.

She gestured.

"Are you serious?"

"Yes, very serious."

"Then I don't know what to say. You are being inconsistent."

She nodded.

Not sure whether or not to be humiliated, he put the car in gear and drove back to his house, where, quite formally, they said good night.

There was no question of having to refuse to ride to the Newark airport with Hugo; he had already arranged for a taxi to take Franz and Jeanette and Victoria there by the time they came downstairs the next morning; and when it came to the door, about eight-thirty, he paid the fare to the driver, and also tipped him, enough so that he could also instruct him to park and help them onto the plane. The Cuttlers were getting ready at the same time, and so there was a great deal of confusion in the front hall, bringing luggage down, carrying it outside, finding wraps, saying good-by. And then, just as Franz and Jeanette were about to leave, Miriam appeared.

She came downstairs, accompanied by Monique. Franz, who had been looking for her repeatedly but had not asked if she was coming (and Hugo wouldn't have known anyway, or Ann been sure), saw her first, over his shoulder. He had the baby's bed in his hands, and, carrying it, he advanced to the foot of the stairs.

"Mother," he said.

She descended to the ground floor, reaching out to touch the top of his head on her way. "Of course," she replied.

They kissed. She kissed Jeanette and Victoria, too, and waved to them all from the door, with the bitter air rushing through into the house. Although she was not dressed, was only in her robe, nobody told her to take care.

"How easily things end, after all," she said to Ann. She was not smiling. She looked drawn, possibly even ill.

And then came the problem of packing the Cuttlers' station wagon so that they could leave for Washington, where they were expected for lunch. Hugo threw himself into it, particularly the question of how to stack in Billy's new bicycle. He supervised, indeed did, one entire packing, then didn't like the looks of it, thought the visibility would be hampered for Bruce up front, and removed everything so that he could do it again; but at this point Bruce intervened. He told Hugo to go up to the house; he and Billy would do it themselves. In a shorter time, therefore, the car was ready, and Ann and Bruce said good-by to her parents.

For no particular reason, for she hadn't had a good time, little Lucy cried. Nobody else did.

Hugo stood on the stoop, Miriam behind him, waving. As the station wagon backed out of the driveway, he went down the steps, and slowly down the walk toward the street, waving, waving, waving, toward the faces in the windows, the fluttering hands. He watched it out of sight, then turned back to the house. The front door still stood open, but Miriam was already gone. He climbed the steps, went inside, looked around. Yes, she had disappeared.

And then he saw Monique. She was on the landing. It seemed she could be waiting.

He called to her. "Are you going out or will you be here this morning?"

"I will probably be here. Unless . . ." She didn't finish.

"Perhaps I will want coffee later. I am going now to

work in my study. If I want an interruption, I will call you, and if you are here, you can come down and join me."

She nodded. "If I am here," she said.

"Naturally, if you go out you can't join me."

"And I may go out," she said.

He nodded, then turned and left her there, hovering, as it were, between his floor and Miriam's.